# MAN FALLING OFF CLIFF

Marion Preece was born and bred in Swansea but now shares a two hundred year old cottage in Garnant, at the foot of the Black Mountain with three cats, two dogs and one husband. She started writing at Swansea Spirit about fifteen years ago and recently graduated from the University of Wales Swansea with a first class honours degree in English. A founder member of *Hookers' Pen*, Marion's stories have appeared in various publications. She has written two books for children and is currently at work on a science fiction novel for adults.

Marion is terrified of snakes, heights and ventriloquists' dummies. She still misses the sound of seagulls.

# Man Falling Off Cliff

Marion Preece

First published in 2008
by YouWriteOn.com
www.youwriteon.com

©Marion Preece

ISBN 978-0-9556500-7-9

Cover photograph and design: Len Preece
Edited by Anna Smith and Emily Hinshelwood
Typeset in Garamond by Emily Hinshelwood


The author asserts the moral right under the Copyright, Designs and Patents Act 1988 to be identified as the author of this work.

All Rights reserved. No part of this publication may be reproduced, stored in a retrieval system, or transmitted, in any form or by any means without the prior written consent of the author, nor be otherwise circulated in any form of binding or cover other than that in which it is published and without a similar condition being imposed on the subsequent purchaser.

*For Len*

## Acknowledgements

With thanks to:

Anna Smith and Emily Hinshelwood, my friends and co-founders of *Hookers' Pen*, who acted as midwives to this collection of short stories. Without their coaxing, bullying and expert assistance this book would not have been born.

My fellow Hookers: Hillary Wickers, Beth Morgan, Sandra Mackness and Sally Spedding for their encouragement and brilliant feedback.

Two enthusiastic and supportive friends, PennyAnne Windsor and Peter Thabit Jones for refining the rough.

And last but not least, to Len for his patient support and endless cups of tea.

'Speaking in Tongues' has previously been published by Honno in the anthology, *My Cheating Heart,* and 'Double Double' has recently been published in *Blue Tattoo.*

# Contents

| | |
|---|---:|
| Introduction | 11 |
| Speaking in Tongues | 13 |
| Brank Ursine | 22 |
| Reckon it's Karma | 25 |
| Swimming in Honey | 31 |
| Rose Diabolo | 35 |
| Man Falling off Cliff | 43 |
| Fast Friendly Service | 45 |
| Biddy | 56 |
| Promontory | 61 |
| Tiger Lily Flames | 65 |
| Away with the Fairies | 67 |
| Double Double | 72 |
| Stones of Tomorrow | 75 |
| Grey Snakes | 81 |
| Rainbows of Maui | 86 |
| Sailing By | 95 |
| Once Bitten | 101 |

# Introduction

I first read some of Marion's short stories several years ago, and I was instantly struck by their refreshing originality and her gutsy use of language. To quote the American writer Robert Frost, there is 'a careful casualness' to her craft. One is easily pulled in to a story by her, totally engaged, and then only on re-reading does one see 'the wires working the magic'; and that is the mark of a very skilled writer.

She achieves the unity of purpose and the unity of construction that are required in a successful short story. There is a perfect harmony of form, content, manner, and intention in her work. She understands the importance of the form's immediacy of effect. Her vision is mature and she pulls back the known curtain of daily life to reveal worlds that are surreal, nightmarish, humorous and, ultimately, uplifting.

Marion is a natural storyteller and with each story she gathers the reader around the campfire of her creation, rewarding them with her ability to gain and sustain their attention via a strong plot, settings that evoke a true sense of place, convincing characters and realistic dialogue.

I gladly recommend this excellent collection of stories to readers interested in compelling and inspired writing. Marion deserves recognition for her gifts throughout Wales and beyond.

Peter Thabit Jones<br>
October, 2008

## SPEAKING IN TONGUES

'Yes, that's it,' Larry whispered urgently. He furtively checked the living room door before easing down his zipper and pressing himself into the soft cushions of the sofa.

Manoeuvring the phone against his jaw, his hands gloated over the velvet of his trousers in counter rhythm to the beat of the music from upstairs. As his breathing quickened, he stared unseeing into the round eyes of Little Tony, sitting opposite him. The jester doll seemed to leer in collusion as the man made a soft, agonised noise.

In the ensuing silence, Larry heard the sound of familiar footsteps.

'Linda, I've got to go,' he said quickly and replaced the phone.

He was leaning forward to pick a stray thread from the dummy's jacket, when something hard struck him on the shoulder. Gritting his teeth with irritation, he turned to face his wife.

'What do you think?' Babs pirouetted in front of him in a cloud of blue net and playfully tapped him again with her fairy wand.

He glanced at the roll of fat protruding from her tight bodice and averted his eyes.

'You look fabulous,' he said, and his gaze shifted to catch the glassy, incredulous stare of Little Tony.

She smiled with relief. 'Really?'

No not really, Babs, he thought. With her faded, brown hair and garish stage make-up, she bore little resemblance to the shy young woman he'd talent-spotted all those years ago. She still had the voice of course, but everything else had gone south. Although - Larry tried to be honest with himself - the punters still liked her, even if they didn't seem so keen on *him* any more. But all that was going to change when he teamed up with the luscious Linda.

'Yeah, really fabulous,' he drawled and cursed himself as he saw that she'd caught the sarcasm. She was fat, not stupid.

Babs went to the mirror, anxiously scrutinising her reflection and Larry felt a tiny flicker of shame. But then she turned, and her sadness had been replaced with sudden gaiety and graceful, theatrical gestures.

'Tony darling, aren't you the handsome one? Come to Babs, let me look at you!'

The small, wooden figure was swept from the cushions and into the air where it was whirled up and around. The doll's eyebrows jiggled madly and its jaw clacked open into a surprised gape.

'You stupid cow, you're going to damage it!' Larry leapt to his feet and grabbed her by the arm.

Babs stumbled to a halt. 'For God's sake, Larry! It was only a bit of fun.'

'Do you know how much we'd have to shell out to replace him?' Seething with irritation, he lowered the dummy into its case and snapped it shut.

Babs rubbed her arm and glared back. 'And who saves us money by repairing and maintaining him?'

Conceding that she had saved them a packet over the years, and also aware of the fact that they had a show in an hour, he clumsily tried to placate her.

'Aw, come on sweetheart, don't take any notice of me - I'm just in a funny mood that's all.'

He lifted his stick with the bells and shook it in her face. 'I say, I say, I say - my dog has no nose!'

Babs dutifully struck a pose, but her voice was flat. 'Your dog has no nose? How does he smell?'

A muffled voice came from the case. 'Awful!'

'We'd better get a move on,' she said and went to get her coat.

Larry slowly packed his jester's hat and stick into his rucksack along with his bottle of Scotch. He stared uneasily at the case. He hadn't spoken - he was going to but ...

*Speaking in Tongues*

The club was half-empty and the punters were not responding well to Larry's new routine.

'Hey, Little Tony!' somebody shouted. 'You look a right state in that outfit - and your dummy looks even worse!'

Larry, perspiring in his velvet suit, tried to laugh, but another voice yelled, 'you'd look much better outside, mate!'

Larry thought uneasily that the hecklers were getting a better response than he was. He glanced over to the corner where Linda sat with her friends. Her blonde hair cascaded over one shoulder of her tight, green sweater as she giggled into her hand. Suddenly conscious of his eyes, she sat up and licked her lips at him.

Babs brought a glass and Larry started the 'bottle of beer' routine - usually a favourite with the punters.

'Gockle a geer! Gockle a geer!'

The familiar taunt had an unusually spiteful sound. A loud raspberry made the crowd roar and perspiration trickled into Larry's eyes as he fought to regain control.

Then a voice yelled, 'gerroff, you boring old twat!'

Larry's voice was drowned out by catcalls and, in panic, he launched into a Morris dance with Little Tony flopping and bouncing about in his arms. The heckling increased in volume, Larry heel-slid in some spilled beer and suddenly, a well-aimed pork pie caught him in the eye.

Babs cut the music and walked forward, admonishing the culprit with her wand.

'Didn't your mother teach you not to play with your food?' she asked teasingly.

The man called out. 'Grant us a wish, Blue Fairy.'

Babs put a finger coquettishly to her cheek. 'Now what can that be?'

The heckler pointed at Larry, who was slinking towards the wings. 'Wave your magic wand, love, and make that silly sod disappear!'

'How about a song instead?' Babs laughed, and several of the regulars clapped as her voice began to weave its magic.

Larry tore at his nails as he glared from the wings. Tonight had been all her fault; she hadn't been quick enough with the props or her responses, and now here she was, grabbing the limelight again. He turned as he heard a clatter of high heels.

'Larry darling,' Linda breathed. Her mouth sucked at his while her hand determinedly groped his crotch. Stupid, irritating bitch! He pushed her away and held her at arms' length.

'Look Linda, I've decided to give us a trial run tonight.'

Her eyes widened but he rushed on. 'Do exactly as we rehearsed. Go back to your table and when I give the signal, come up on stage.'

Fifteen minutes later, Babs came into the tiny dressing room and stooped down in front of the cracked mirror.

'You okay, Lar?'

She bent over and yards of net puffed up, wafting her heavy odour towards him. Faugh! It was no wonder he couldn't get it up for her any more. After half a bottle of Scotch, he didn't even bother to hide a grimace of distaste as his eyes met hers in the mirror.

'Mmm.' The voice sounded as though it had just licked something delectable.

'What?' Larry jerked around.

Babs looked at him strangely. 'I didn't say anything.' She spat on her palms and started easing out the wrinkles in her tights.

'Tasty.' The word was sibilant and mocking.

Little Tony, propped upright on the chair, was staring straight at Larry and as he watched, one eyelid clicked down in a lascivious wink.

'The doll ...' Larry pointed to Little Tony with a trembling finger.

Babs opened the hatch on the back of the dummy and tutted as she fiddled with the mechanism. 'I thought I'd fixed this. You'll just have to put extra pressure on the control knob for tonight and I'll sort it out tomorrow.'

The hecklers had gone and a new crowd had filtered into the hall during the break. Seemingly determined to have a good time, they groaned at all the old jokes and laughed at Little Tony's antics. Larry glowed - he was back on form.

'And now, ladies and gentlemen ... '

Babs stepped forward.

'We have a change to our programme!' Larry bared his teeth in a feral grin that stopped Babs in her tracks.

'As a professional entertainer, I am always on the lookout for exciting new talent. So this evening,' Larry's smile glittered as he pointed to Linda, 'I want you to give a warm welcome to an up-and-coming young star ... Miss Linda Forster!'

He glanced sideways and caught Babs staring as Linda scrambled to her feet.

Larry clapped loudly and called out. 'Don't be shy Linda, that's the way. Give her a big hand folks!'

There were a few desultory claps as Linda climbed onto the stage, but then somebody wolf-whistled and Larry felt slippery with success. His eyes sought Babs' - but she had disappeared. He shrugged, easily pushing away a niggling pinch of guilt.

'Ready?' he whispered, pulling Linda around into position in the spotlight. He noted anxiously that her face was set and he could feel her shaking through the thin material of her sweater.

'Say hello to the lady, Tony.'

The dummy's head rotated and its eyebrows waggled. 'Hello lady.' It leaned towards Larry and whispered loudly, 'she's built isn't she?'

This was where Linda should have said: 'You cheeky monkey!' But she seemed mute with fear. In the silence somebody coughed. Larry could smell his own sweat as he brought Little Tony close to Linda and made it roll its eyes.

What happened next he could never explain. His throat clicked as he started to project: 'Have you got a sister at home?' But what came out of Tony's mouth was: 'Hey, lady - are those knockers real?'

Then somehow, the dummy's head was swinging around to stare into Larry's horrified face.

A man in the audience guffawed as Linda's eyes slowly turned to the dummy.

'You cheeky bugger,' she said. 'Sod off!'

Larry's fingers fell away from the controls in Little Tony's body, but the doll continued to move. The laughter of the audience washed over him, and Larry's teeth began to chatter as he heard the dummy say: 'I'd like to give you one, Linda. Right now on this table.'

The audience gasped, waiting for her reply.

Linda tossed her hair and examined her nails. 'Sorry Little Tony, I'm not into wooden ... legs.'

Larry gaped at her through bulging eyes. That was fast for her - the little bitch was enjoying herself!

The whole audience was laughing now as Linda slipped her sweater off one shoulder and fluffed up her hair.

Moaning, Larry twisted his head towards the darkness of the wings, searching frantically for Babs.

The dummy waggled its head. 'Larry tells me that he's always hard; always ready for it.'

Linda snorted. 'You've got to be joking!'

Little Tony's eyebrows shot up and the crowd roared laughing. Larry glared at Linda, but she was totally immersed in the dummy.

'Bit of a limp rag is he?' The dummy leaned against Linda's shoulder and batted its eyelids. 'I bet you wish that *he* had a wooden ... leg.'

Larry was trapped. The noises of the club faded and he hissed with fear as Little Tony's voice boomed and receded in his head. Spots of light began to obscure his vision and the acrid taste of vomit rose in his throat.

'Shall we let these folks into a little secret, Linda?'

Linda nodded happily.

'Shall we tell them that Larry is always on the prowl for naïve little tarts like you? Especially the ones that give good ... telephone.'

Linda's smile faded as Little Tony peeled back its lips in a hideous grin. 'But I'm afraid he also likes his meat young and fresh, and from the smell of you, love, I'd say you're well past your sell-by date.'

The laughter in the hall petered out as Linda began to cry, but the chirpy voice continued.

'Aw look - it's upset! Well, give it a big round of applause, folks.

It's not very bright, but you can see why he'd prefer it to saggy old Babs.'

Several people booed, Linda ran off the stage and the props table crashed sideways as Larry's head hit the floor.

Eight months later, on the advice of his psychiatrist, Larry attempted a reconciliation with his wife. After several fruitless phone calls, Babs agreed to meet him at the theatre where she would be working.

The Alhambra was busy as he walked around to the stage door and was directed to her dressing room. Smoothing back his hair, he took a deep breath and knocked on the door. At first he thought he had the wrong room, then his jaw dropped.

'Babs?'

She looked fabulous! Her hair was darker and shone in the light as she moved. Her makeup was flawless and her figure …

'Come in, Larry. I've been expecting you.' Babs turned and he blinked at the way her black, beaded gown clung to her generous curves.

She sat down and began to apply lip-gloss with brisk movements.

'How are you, Larry?'

He swallowed. 'It's good to see you.' He tore his eyes away from her and glanced nervously around.

'What do you want?'

He coughed, checked around the room again and said, 'I'm better now.'

'And your point is?'

'I think we could make a go of it again.'

Babs smiled at him through the glass. 'This is a one woman show, Larry.'

She was laughing at him but he forced himself to relax as he'd been taught.

'I thought maybe the position of manager? You owe me, Babs.'

'Alright.'

'What?'

She turned to face him. 'I said alright. I need someone who knows the business and it might as well be you.' She rose to her feet and his eyes flickered greedily from her face to her breasts.

'Make yourself comfortable until the show has finished,' she said. 'And then we'll go over details. There's whisky in the cupboard.'

Larry checked every corner and niche in the room before settling down with the bottle.

'So, for one night only, please welcome ... our very own ... Barbara Mandrell!'

As the small loudspeaker in the corner relayed the compere's voice, Larry gulped down his drink. Thunderous applause died down as Babs began to sing and he listened intently to her rich voice. Why had he never realized how talented she was?

Three glasses of whisky later, he leapt up, punching the air with excitement.

'Larry boy, you've landed on your feet!'

Wrenching open the door, he weaved his way over to the wings.

He was watching the show with a dreamy smile on his face when he heard the voice of his nightmares.

'I've been waiting for you, Larry.'

His bowels turned to water as a grinning face appeared around the curtain.

Babs' voice soared as Larry backed away, babbling. 'No! You're not real! I've had treatment for this and you're not real!'

'Shut up, Larry. You always did talk a load of shit.' Little Tony seemed to float towards him.

A distant, rational part of Larry's mind knew this couldn't be right, and his eyes searched for hidden wires as the dummy closed in, wafting the smell of oil, and something ... else.

'Hey, Larry. Wanna see something really scary?'

Larry's eyes bulged with horror as its lips receded, revealing a crooked row of razor-sharp teeth that glinted wickedly in the half-light.

He turned to run, when pain exploded in his leg. Thunderous applause drowned out the sound of his screams as he fled out into the night.

Babs took her final bow and made her way over to the gloom of the wings. Pushing aside the curtain, she saw the small figure slumped forward, in a child's wicker chair. She laughed softly as her fingers moved over the buttons of a slim control box and Little Tony, immaculate in a white tuxedo, snapped upright. The dummy's jaw clacked open and shut as a hidden recorder replayed - 'So long, sucker!'

Because of the size of Larry's ego, her talent for mimicry and throwing her voice had been kept under wraps. Once however, out of boredom, she had impersonated Linda over the phone. It had been mildly distasteful.

She'd known that Larry wouldn't be able to resist coming down to watch, and it was a pity that she hadn't been there to witness the look on his face, but there, you couldn't have everything.

The audience was calling for an encore, and as she turned, she paused momentarily to frown at some dark red splashes on the floor in front of her. At that moment, the orchestra started to play, so, lifting the hem of her gown, she gingerly stepped over the sticky mess.

She walked back into the spotlight and began to sing.

## Brank Ursine

With some difficulty Mrs. Vallon coaxed, poked and shoved her stomach into a pair of skinny, wet-look jeans. She regarded her reflection. What was below was now above, billowing over the waistband like an overenthusiastic soufflé. Her ample breasts wobbled precariously over the lace of her balcony bra as she searched through her wardrobe, emerging triumphant in a leopard-print blouse with tiny angel sleeves. Deodorant clouded the air as she bent down to do up her new, high-heeled sandals. Her back winced and the jeans cut her unmentionables uncomfortably, but she felt, she hoped she looked ... not bad.

The garden centre was busy as she casually weaved her way through the roses, dark glasses on alert.

'Hello, hello.' A gangly man with thinning hair stood at her side.

'Oh, hello Stan.' Her reply was less than enthusiastic, but he grinned with delight.

'What's it to be today, then? Endangered Victorian roses? Genoese oak dovecote? Argantua Sunfish?'

She blushed. 'Brank Ursine.'

He scratched his neck. 'Brank Ursine, Brank Ursine. Nope - you got me again, Mrs. Vallon.'

'Oh, dear,' she said, looking crestfallen.

'Better call the expert then?'

'So kind.'

She winced as he bellowed over the heads of customers, 'Daniel!'

A muscular young man with the face of an angel appeared from behind a today-only offer of three-conifers-for-the-price-of-two. The twitch at the corner of her eye duelled with the pounding of her heart

*Brank Ursine*

as he walked, as though in slow motion, towards her.

His vest was very white and he was very tanned. There was a glint of silver at his wrist as he raked back unruly hair from his face. Her breathing quickened and she felt as moist as the pot of begonias that her fingers were dabbling in.

'Mrs. Vallon! How lovely to see you again. And so soon.' His teeth gleamed in the sun. 'May I say how wonderful you look today?'

She flushed, prettily she hoped, and shifted discreetly, trying to ease the flossing action of her jeans.

'Ever heard of Brank Ursine, Daniel?' Stan briskly re-potted the begonia.

Daniel gazed into the distance and repeated, 'Brank Ursine.'

She stared at his mouth, at his throat, at his Adam's apple that went up and down as he spoke.

'Brank Ursine, or Bear's Breach, a member of the Acanthus family, used widely in the old days and mentioned favourably in 'Culpepper's Herbal' as a cure for many ailments.'

'My word, Daniel,' said Stan, straightening up and wiping his hands on his overall. 'That's amazing that is. Never fails to amaze us, does he Mrs. Vallon?'

'No,' she said.

Daniel produced a mobile phone from his back pocket and wandered back and fore, talking. She watched his taut buttocks, his hand on his narrow hip, the dirt under his fingernails - good dirt though, fine, not nasty. She could feel those hands on her. And his mouth. And his hips. My goodness, it was hot in here!

Stan walked over to talk to an elderly couple arguing over tomato plants, and Daniel came back. She sighed.

'Right, Mrs. Vallon. I've been through to our plant finder and they say that Brank Ursine can only be found in Norway.' He looked deep into her eyes as he named the price. And caught her arm to steady her as she fell off one of her sandals. He smiled.

'I must have it,' she heard herself say.

'Of course,' he murmured, with breath that smelled of hot apples.

A fortnight later, cut and blow-dried and wearing pixie boots with a flower-sprigged mini dress that had to be tugged down every fourth step, she drove to the garden centre. Stan was there. Daniel was not.

'Been fired,' said Stan cheerfully. 'Crafty young devil was creaming off the profits with his partner.'

'Partner?' she squeaked.

'Yeah, bloke at Plant Finders.'

He looked at her face. 'But I got your Brank Ursine here.' He proudly produced a squat, sad-looking plant with dirty-white flowers.

She looked at the plant. She looked at Stan. She wrote a cheque.

'Thank you,' she said.

Mrs. Vallon, unseeing, wandered into the pet care centre next door. Amongst the red-shirted staff was a young man with blonde dreadlocks ... wearing a suit.

Mrs. Vallon decided that what she really needed was an exotic pet. Or two.

## Reckon it's Karma

'Crapulence!'

Geoffrey Whittlestone, grimly ignoring the sound of bongo drums coming from the windows above, muttered the word over and over as he trudged down the stone steps leading from the ground floor flat, and carried the slopping watering can across the garden.

It was against the rules of the housing association to plant any flowers; only grass was allowed on the small square of earth that was the front garden. But Geoffrey had given one of his hard looks in response to the raised eyebrows of the council gardener and the man, with amazing speed, had scrubbed his mower over the lawn before driving off.

In a moment of uncharacteristic rebellion the previous winter, Geoffrey had purchased a small, dried-up rose, on sale at Woolworths. Tangled amongst other rejects in a cardboard box, it had been no more than two brown twigs; but it was the picture that had caught his eye - a deep-red rose of unbearable beauty, bearing the name 'Julia'. He had bought a box of bone meal and, back at the house, had read the instructions on the packet several times before digging a deep hole and filling it with water. He had tended the rose every morning and again at sunset and it had come to life before his eyes. Tiny bumps swelled and unfurled into glossy, green leaves and he had watched the formation of the single bud with all the delighted intensity of a lover.

On Tuesday the bud had started to split, allowing a tantalising glimpse of reddish-pink interior, and this morning it should just about be starting to unfold. But Geoffrey wouldn't look. Not yet. Like a child savouring a present for as long as possible, he kept his eyes on the darkening circle of earth. Eventually, unable to contain himself any longer, he placed the watering can to one side and straightened, allowing his eyes to trail ever so slowly upwards, consuming each curve, lingering on every shiny leaf until he reached the top. As he stared at the bare stalk, his smile died.

'Oy, oy, Geoff!'

Terry was poised theatrically in the doorway to the top flat. His face was scrubbed and shining and the ever-present, idiotic smile set Geoffrey's teeth on edge.

'Whatcha think then, me old mate? Scrub up alright don't I?' The young man swaggered towards him, proudly smoothing his hands down his chest.

Geoffrey barely registered the baggy, pinstriped trousers, the canary yellow waistcoat or the Jesus sandals. The Julia rose was just as he had pictured it. Deep crimson, velvet petals just beginning to unfold - perfection. It was pinned to Terry's chest.

'Got the trousers in Oxfam for one-twenty-five, the waistcoat in the Red Cross sale for fifty pee - 'cos of the stain - and the rose was for free, courtesy of the council. Beauty innit?' Terry bent his head and sniffed deeply in appreciation. 'You did a good job looking after this Geoff, if it was left up to that lot it wouldn't have survived into June.'

Geoffrey's fists clenched and his eyes narrowed to slits as Terry boxed him on the arm and danced away. He hadn't allowed himself to lose his temper since he'd left the hospital, but now all his pent-up anger focussed on the clownish figure prancing in front of him. His hand shot out - to grab the rose or to punch Terry on the nose he couldn't say - just as his housemate swooped down to hoist up the watering can.

Geoffrey's momentum carried him around and he stumbled. Terry shot out a steadying arm and laughed in admiration. 'Whoa there, Geoff. Shouldn't be doing acrobatics at your age!'

Again Geoffrey threw out his hand, only to have it grabbed and pumped.

'I know you're busy, mate and haven't got time and all that, but thanks for your help with the speech.' The young man spread his arms and grinned widely. 'It's great you and me sharing the same house innit? Liking the same things - music and that - looking out for each other, like. Reckon it's Karma. Here look, I made this for you.' His fingers fumbled with something at Geoffrey's wrist and Geoffrey, blind with fury, struggled to get free.

'Anyway, shit, gotta go - don't want to keep Lyn and Davy waiting. Never been a best man before. Never been to a wedding come to think of it. You take it easy today old mate, it's gonna be a scorcher. Put a hat on when you go out. I'll fetch some food home if there's any left. Catch you laterrrr.'

With a final punch to Geoffrey's shoulder, Terry vaulted the low hedge and loped off.

Geoffrey's hands shook as he stared at his violated rose bush. He was sick to bloody death of Terry. 'Old mate' this and 'old dear' that - he was only fifty-four for God's sake and he was certainly not Terry's mate.

The top flat had been empty for over a year, and during that time Geoffrey had been able to pretend that the house was theirs and that she had just popped out to the shop. His days were pleasantly filled with tidying and re-arranging the furniture or with trips to the library to read the papers and to expand his vocabulary by learning a new word every day. Yesterday's word had been 'crapulence'. The monastic silence and solitude had served him well until Terry had exploded into his life three months ago.

Despite elaborate rituals to avoid him, the young idiot, having misread Geoffrey's forced politeness as overtures of friendship, had adopted him as some sort of surrogate father figure. Just the previous evening he had insisted on reading out the inane words of his best man's speech, all of it, even though Geoffrey had pointedly kept him standing outside the door. The grammar had been atrocious and the words had been filled with new-age psychobabble, all soul mates, dolphins and the universe.

Geoffrey grabbed his jacket and headed into town. To add to his fury, the council office was closed and his arguments as to why Terry should be evicted from the flat - loud music, pestering him at inconvenient times for sugar or advice on how to change a fuse, not to mention his hippy friends on the stairs at all hours of the day and night, went round and around in his mind as he stomped, head down, through the busy streets. Suddenly his head snapped up as he caught a whiff of rotting seaweed and hot dogs.

The seafront was full of screeching holidaymakers and the glare coming off the water hurt his eyes, but he stubbornly waded along the soft sand until he found a secluded spot. Peeling off his jacket he mentally berated yet another council official, a woman this time, as he banged his shoe against a rock. He was wiping his handkerchief across his forehead when a bright flash of colour fluttering at his wrist made him frown. Lifting his hand to his face, he stared stupidly at the neatly fashioned string bracelet. Red and yellow, it had tiny, purple beads threaded in here and there.

'Terry.'

Geoffrey pulled at the dangling strings. They had tried to coax him to make these in hospital - what did they call them? Friendship bracelets. He picked and fiddled with increasing agitation but the bracelet would not budge. The winking beads made him think of funeral wreaths, sleeping tablets and Julia. He began to feel sick. A family with young children were walking towards him and he got to his feet. He would cut the damned thing off later.

As he trudged along, the beach stretched away like the long years ahead of him. 'You want to be careful at your age, old mate.' Geoffrey's feet stomped holes in the sand. Suddenly his stride faltered and he stopped. To the left was the start of a high cliff and a rush of the same feeling that had prompted him to buy the rose made his throat swell. He reached the base in four long strides and after a beat of hesitation started to climb. He ascended with a smooth rhythm, for the first time in years exulting in the power of his body and acutely aware of himself as a man.

The first rush of euphoria pushed him rapidly upwards, there were many easy handholds and his feet slipped neatly into well placed crevices. Julia's face floated above him and the promise in her smile urged him on. It was only when his foot slipped and the rock-face slammed into his cheek that he became aware of the wind that was pushing him sideways. He looked down to see the beach far below and the feeling of peace vanished to be replaced with abject terror.

'Oh you stupid bugger!' Hugging the rock he looked up to see the top of the cliff, just a few feet away. He forced himself to move but his foot slipped again. Throwing his hand up in one last despairing lunge, his right hand made contact with blessed earth and grass, but the earth began to crumble and his fingers had become stiff, alien things that would not grip. His terrified gaze slipped down from his white knuckles and came to rest on the garish cotton bracelet. As the wind whipped the ends, they danced like the tails of a kite.

'Sorry,' he whispered as the panic subsided to be replaced with astonishing calm. 'I'm so sorry. I wish ... ' He allowed his fingers to open.

'Blimey Geoff! Thought you said you couldn't make it. Took the scenic route did you?' A grinning face appeared over the top and a strong hand reached down to grip his wrist.

Geoffrey lay sprawled on sheep-cropped grass, gulping in the blessed blueness of the sky. He raised his head to see ten or twelve colourfully-dressed people sitting around a small fire. One girl wore a deep red rose in her hair. They were all gaping at him.

Terry opened his arms. 'Everyone this is Geoff, my mate from the house, not afraid of nothing or nobody is Geoff. Came up this cliff like firkin' Spiderman he did!'

Amidst the babble of greetings and approval, a smacking kiss was planted on his lips, a large paper cup thrust into his shaking hands and the group resumed laughing and eating.

Terry beamed as Geoffrey drank deeply without stopping, then ambled over to the fire. Geoffrey propped himself on one elbow and tried to focus on a man with a white ponytail who had started strumming a guitar. A lanky lad - the groom Geoff presumed because of the crown of daisies on his head - flopped down beside him.

'Glad to meet you at last, Geoff; any friend of Terry's has to be sound. He's a good kid, considering his upbringing.'

Davy, Geoffrey remembered the name with muzzy triumph,

smiled and passed him a thin cigarette. Geoffrey wrinkled his nose in bewilderment but, despite having given up over a year ago, took a polite puff.

'Can't think why myself, Geoff, but our Terry thinks the sun shines out of your arse.'

Geoffrey turned to stare at the younger man but Davy gently retrieved the strange cigarette and smiled into the sun.

The ocean had begun to turn an amazing blue when Davy clapped him on the shoulder and got to his feet. 'Right then mate, let's get you a plate of sausages. More wine? Better had - we're going skinny-dipping in a bit.'

The moon glinted on Geoffrey's glasses as he tripped lightly down the steps with his watering can. Water slopped over his feet, the grass tickled his toes and he put a reproving finger against his lips to suppress irrepressible giggles. He lay belly down on the cool earth and rested his chin on his hands. Julia was regal and mysterious in the moonlight, and he was not at all surprised to see two tiny buds, just beginning to form.

## SWIMMING IN HONEY

I came across the silly thing while I was looking for envelopes in his desk. It was poetry of a sort and in his handwriting, which I thought strange. George had always scoffed at anything even mildly creative as being written by 'queers' who should have three years in the Guards in order to sort them out. It was a draft copy with lots of crossings out: 'Her eyes like lasers' (something) 'my soul' (something, something) 'strong' (crossings out) 'my life' (lots of crossings out) 'golden' (something) 'my wife.'

I wondered if he was becoming bi-polar. It's on his side of the family you know, cousin Alfred to be exact - impossible man. But then it struck me. Valentine's day was just around the corner. Could it be that he was composing a verse for me? We had never acknowledged the wretched day but he had been acting strangely of late.

I should mention here that George and I were never compatible, not in that way. If I were to be honest, the death rattle of our sexual relations began on our wedding night. George was an earth shaker if you catch my drift and I was a slow burner, so our marriage in that sense was a disaster. But otherwise we were well-suited. Having both been brought up to make the best of things, we brushed all intimacy under the duvet like an embarrassing damp stain and got on with our lives.

George is a successful businessman with offices in London and Bath. When he is home we go to the theatre, attend dinner parties or just stay in and relax. Four or five times a year we holiday with mutual friends who regard us as the perfect couple.

For myself, I am neither ecstatic nor depressed. My life is a measured walk along a promenade of respectability. Every weekday morning I leave instructions for dinner and go to the gym. In the afternoon I might meet a friend, have my hair textured or pop into Harrods. If George is at home, we'll have dinner and talk about our day before he retires to his study. I generally curl up on the sofa and read, or write a few letters until it's time for bed; and if my dreams turn black, well all I have to do is take one of my little pills and I'm back on an even keel.

But last week, to my alarm, George suggested a trip to St. Lucia for 'some quality time'. I was appalled. 'It's too early in the season,' I said. 'None of our crowd will be there.'

'We need to talk,' he said.

As usual I was right, there was absolutely nobody there that we knew. When we arrived at our hotel, I suggested lunch and we sat at a table overlooking the bay. It really was beautiful and I was longing to be in the water. George only had a salad as we had planned to go snorkelling later.

'It will be an opportunity to try out the new camera,' he said.

He took no salt as lately he has been looking after his weight and his heart. 'You'll get cramp,' I warned and offered him my lasagne. George so hates waste.

Moonlight glittered over the waters of the bay as we swam out, much further than we intended really, but we had done it many times before and were both strong swimmers. George had the camera strapped to his wrist and managed to photograph a number of unusual marine species. But then he started to feel unwell and we had begun to turn back when he doubled up with cramp.

As I floated lazily on my back I recalled the conversation in our room earlier.

'I'm glad we could be civilized about this,' George had said as he briskly re-capped his pen and put away the papers. 'We've let it drag on for far too long. I have arranged for you to get twenty per cent of the business plus the town house. I think that is fair. We can still be friends.'

*Swimming in Honey*

The flash of the camera ricocheted through the depths as my foot shoved his head further down. I had despaired of the potency of the crushed pills, even though he had bolted down every morsel of the lasagne, so the cramp was a gift from God.

'I managed to decipher your poem, George,' I said, as I prised his fingers from my ankle. 'I had some help from a very nice young man in that computer shop towards the lower end of Oxford Street. I'm afraid I was consumed by curiosity when Valentine's Day arrived and there was no love note from you. Yes George, you can smile, I know I was being uncharacteristically whimsical, but there you go.' I felt one of his fingers break and his grip loosened.

'Anyway, I wasn't sure if they could do anything, but it's quite unnerving what technology can achieve these days. The poem ... should we call it that do you think? - oh, alright, for the sake of argument, let's - is dedicated 'to Jessica'. That's your new PA isn't it? The one with the hip bones, who is young enough to be your granddaughter? Sweet. Now let me see, how did it go?'

George's body rose again, his hands clawing for the surface. I twisted easily and kicked at his face with my heel.

'"Her eyes are lasers but you see my soul/ You make me strong, she drains my life/ I'll die of thirst if I can't drink/ The golden honey from your shrine."'

'You never even bothered to track down the source of my honey, did you George?' I said. 'But I digress, where was I? Oh, yes. This is the best bit, listen: "I'm asking you my darling love/ I'm begging you to be my wife."'

I kicked him in the face again. 'It doesn't even scan, you treacherous bastard!'

His body sank for the last time and a shoal of neon fish scattered at the descending flashes of light.

I swam back towards the lights of the shore in a leisurely breaststroke, the water a soothing swathe of silk against my body.

Please don't misunderstand me; I was indifferent to the fact that George had found himself yet another mistress. I didn't give a jot as long as he was discreet. What I couldn't stomach was that this time I would be publicly humiliated and I simply couldn't have that.

Strolling out of the surf, I took time to smooth back my hair before I began to call for help.

## Rose Diabolo

Doris had bought the black leather bag on ebay for five pounds.

'Bit big, isn't it?' Arthur had peered at her over his glasses.

'But it's nice, don't you think?' She twirled, showing it off to its best advantage. 'Arthur? Classy, like.'

He shrugged and returned to the sports pages.

Although secretly startled by its size, Doris was entranced with the myriad of zips and compartments, and it had kept her amused for the whole of the previous day finding suitable places for her purse, house keys, mobile phone, diary, notebook, pens, sudoku book, reading glasses and tissues. It had a carrying handle as well as a shoulder strap and she had discovered a cunning slot for her folding umbrella on one side.

Alright, it was heavy and made her shoulder ache, but the sheer size seemed to empower her, making her fantasize about being a solicitor or an accountant coming home from the office instead of a housewife, going to visit her husband's aunt in a retirement home in Bridgend.

'Why don't you come with me today Arthur?' she asked hopefully.

'Nah,' he said with a shudder. 'I can't stand those places - they smell. You go.'

On impulse, she'd put on a white blouse and black gypsy skirt instead of her usual flowered dress and cardigan. She didn't have black shoes, but found a pair of flat, navy sling-backs at the back of her wardrobe. They would have to do. She couldn't wear heels anyway with the state of her feet.

'You look like a bloody waitress,' Arthur called after her.

Doris hesitated in the doorway. She didn't know what it was that she was wishing for, but she wished for it with all her heart.

The train slid smoothly out of Swansea, and Doris sat with her hand clutching the bag at her side. Scenery flashed by as she stared out of the window, lost in her daydreams.

'That bag's too big for you,' Arthur's Aunty Ethel said. 'You're too dumpy for a skirt like that and your shoes don't match.'

Doris tried to change the conversation. 'I brought you some Liquorice Allsorts, Aunty. You like these don't you? They're your favourites.'

'No. Can't stand them. Get under my plate they do.' She sniffed and stuffed the despised sweets into her own, roomy handbag.

Doris then spent the afternoon hearing about her sister-in-law's wonderful visit, how beautifully dressed she was and how caring.

'Brought me Thornton's she did, lovely chocolates they were. Expensive.'

Yes, Doris thought, and she visits you once a year, even though she only lives in Cardiff.

'Off to the Boharmas next week. Got a good job, she has.'

Doris smoothed down the folds of her skirt.

The old lady shifted and craned her neck. 'Anyway, they're bringing the tea trolley round now.'

'See you next week then Aunty.'

'If I'm still here.' Aunty Ethel laid her head back against the chair and gave a little cough.

Doris had to fight her way onto the Swansea train and stood with swollen ankles, crushed against a fat businessman with halitosis. As the train slowed for Port Talbot, she spotted an empty seat and flopped down gratefully. An elegantly dressed young woman took the seat opposite and Doris' eyes devoured her expensive business suit with its very short skirt. With one hand the woman impatiently swept back a wing of dark, shining hair and Doris tried not to stare at the long, white-tipped nails. Fabulous.

She gave the young woman a friendly smile, remarked on the weather and offered a mint humbug. The woman regarded her with glacier-blue eyes and, as Doris' smile faded, she took a mobile phone from her bag and began speaking rapidly in French. Doris tried not to look impressed and gazed out of the window at passing steelworks. She remembered few French words from school but imagined herself sitting at a Parisian pavement café, waving a languid arm at her lover.

'Bonjour,' she said in her mind's eye. 'Comment ça va?'

Suddenly realizing that she was moving her fingers and mouthing the words, and becoming aware of silence, she turned her head back to see the young woman zipping up the front compartment of her large bag. Doris' face grew hot. She fumbled about at her side and came up with her sudoku book and a pen. Their bags were identical! Stuffing hers under the table she studied a puzzle with deep concentration.

At Neath station, the young woman got out and Doris watched her confident walk until she was out of sight. Feeling small and insignificant, Doris slumped against the seat as the train began moving once again. Soon, familiar landmarks began to appear and she fished around impatiently under the table.

'Come on out, you bugger. Ouch!' Static leapt between her fingers and the handle of the bag. Sucking her hand she levered the bag towards her with her foot. It felt even heavier now but she threw the sudoku and pen inside and got to her feet as the train pulled into Swansea.

Carrying it by the handle, just as the young French woman had done, Doris, head held high, tried to imitate her confident walk while wondering whether the market would have any cockles left to go with the bacon at home for Arthur's tea. Her high heels clicked on the station tiles.

She wobbled and stopped. High heels? She looked down with disbelief at her smart, black court shoes and impossibly slender ankles. What ... ? She closed her eyes. It was hot, she was tired and Aunty Ethel had been a right handful. She opened one eye and squinted down at her old navy sling-backs.

Just then her mobile rang. It had a different ring tone. She stared at the tiny phone in her hand. It was a metallic blue, hers was black.

Oh God! That girl had taken her bag!

'Hello?' she whispered.

'Juliette? C'est moi, Jean Paul.' The man's voice crackled and broke up.

'This is not Juliette, monsieur. Je suis Mrs. Doris Hendy,' she said loudly.

There was a flurry of French interspersed with static.

'Your ami has taken mon bag,' she shouted. 'Mon bag!'

A couple with two children were staring at her. She stumbled out into the sunshine with the phone clamped to her ear.

'What? I can't hear ... '

Abruptly the phone went dead.

Doris heaved the strap onto her shoulder and crossed the busy main road. She'd go to the police station, that's what she'd do. Her footsteps slowed and she came to a halt, tapping the strange bag with curious fingers.

The café was empty and she sat in a window seat, idly toying with one of the zippers and drinking her coffee.

'Espresso, s'il vous plaît.' She had said waving her hand airily. The rather dishy waiter had not responded to her joke.

The first compartment held a slim, embossed make-up bag and, glancing around, Doris took out a gold lipstick case. *Christian Dior*, she read, *Rose Diabolo*. Doris didn't wear make-up. Arthur didn't like it.

'All lipstick and no knickers,' he'd say, watching young women go past in the street.

As she screwed the tube up to its fullest extent, Doris couldn't resist. Taking an oval mirror from the bag, she applied the vibrant colour to her mouth. She pressed her lips together and pouted. Fabulous. She looked around at the waiter and he winked.

Delving into the main compartment she came up with an embroidered cream scarf with silk fringes. Fabulous. She flung the scarf over one shoulder and unzipped another pocket. The graduated sunglasses made her feel exotic and mysterious and gold hoop earrings and bracelets that chinked completed the picture. She turned again, this time more slowly, with her hand resting sensually on the scarf at her shoulder. The waiter's jaw dropped.

She couldn't remember the last time she had had so much fun. She couldn't even use scented soap at home because of Arthur's asthma, but, as she pressed the tiny phial of perfume against her wrist and throat, Doris sighed with bliss.

Different compartments revealed legal-looking papers done up with black ribbon, a diary, annoyingly all in French, a black leather wallet containing what seemed to her to be an awful lot of Euros, car keys and a passport. Juliette Dalmain's face, framed by wings of jet-black hair, stared haughtily back.

Doris patted her own salt and pepper curls and wondered if her hairdresser could cut her hair like that. No harm in asking, though every time she took in a picture from a magazine, she always came out with the same tight perm.

'Oh no Mrs. Hendy,' the girl would say. 'This cut would be too severe for your face.' They both knew what she really meant.

Doris turned and raised a hand. Immediately the waiter appeared at her side. She asked for another espresso and he almost tripped as he hurried away. What on earth was the matter with the boy?

She finished her coffee and as she dabbed away the froth from her upper lip, realized she didn't have any money. Hunched with embarrassment she thought that perhaps she should ring Arthur. With shaking hands she applied another coat of *Rose Diabolo*, then in one smooth movement, adjusted her scarf, took her bag and stood up. The waiter raised an enquiring eyebrow and began to speak rapidly in French.

'No, no,' Doris waved her hands. 'I'm not really French, that earlier was just a little joke.'

The young man shook his head and shrugged.

'My bag was stolen,' she said loudly and slowly. 'On the train coming back from Bridgend.'

The waiter's nostrils flared appreciatively as her perfume wafted towards him.

'I don't have any money to pay,' she began to babble. 'But I'm on my way to the police station and as soon as I get home, I will get some money and come back here and pay for my drinks.' She looked at him expectantly.

He leaned his elbow on the counter, rested his chin on his hand and smiled dreamily. Doris decided that he wasn't quite right in the head and turned to walk out of the door. Immediately the waiter leapt over the counter and caught her arm.

'Non, non, mam'selle!' He shrugged apologetically and made the universal sign for money.

Doris felt her temper rising. She rummaged around in the bag and waved the bundle of Euros in his face. 'Look, you little twerp! This is all I have!'

The waiter hesitated and looked around. Then he smiled, took her fingertips and kissed them. He held the door open for her and ushered her out into the sunshine.

Well! Doris couldn't believe her day. She began to think that perhaps she was dreaming all this and was at this very moment asleep on the train. Determinedly ignoring the sound of high heels clicking on the pavement and the feel of a suit jacket blowing against her chest in the wind, she hurried down Alexandra Road to the police station.

A sergeant stood at the desk working on a crossword. As she marched up to him he smoothly slid the newspaper under a pile of papers before straightening up and sucking in his stomach.

'Bonjour,' he said. 'Est-ce que je peut vous aider?'

Doris clicked her fingers. She had it! 'This is Candid Camera isn't it?' She smiled broadly and wagged her finger at him.

The policeman seemed enchanted and smiled back.

'I've seen this on the telly,' she said. 'I've always ... '

He smiled and gave a Gallic shrug. He was good, she'd give him that.

The phone tinkled in her bag.

'Excuse me,' she murmured and the sergeant inclined his head.

'Yes?' she said curtly.

'Oh, thank God, Juliette,' the voice was familiar and breathless.

'Is this Jean Paul?'

'Yes, who did you think it was you goose?' His laugh was deep and sexy.

'I don't ... ' Doris began. 'I mean ... why couldn't I understand you earlier?'

'I was driving through a poor reception area.'

'Ah!' Doris carefully examined her long, white-tipped nails and tapped them thoughtfully against the desk.

The sergeant looked at her enquiringly and she smiled, touching the tip of her tongue to her lips, feeling it slide against the *Rose Diabolo*. He opened his mouth to speak.

'One moment,' she held up a peremptory hand, causing him to lift an eyebrow.

'Juliette, you know that it's vital to give the papers into George Walters' hands today.'

Doris' voice was unnaturally curt. 'I am all too aware of that, Jean Paul. Through no fault of my own, I got off at the wrong stop. But I'm here now and I'm about to get directions from a very nice policeman.' Doris smiled at the sergeant and he cleared his throat importantly while tidying the papers in front of him.

'Well don't be late, darling. We only have one night in London and we don't want to waste it do we?'

He laughed again and so did she. But this was not Doris' usual barking laugh; this was an unfamiliar, throaty chuckle. She closed the phone with a decisive snap.

Bending down to her bag she saw, with little surprise, that she now wore a very short skirt, and sheer stockings that showed off her shapely legs to their best advantage. A wing of jet-black hair fell across her face as she held out a business card and pointed to the address. The sergeant scratched his head and then his face cleared.

'Oh, right,' he said. 'Now what you have to do is this.' He spoke very slowly and very clearly. 'You go out of here and turn left down the road to the Magistrates' Court. Then you take the second right up the hill and then ... ' He stopped at the incomprehension on her face. 'Tell you what - better call you a taxi.' She looked blankly at him.

'Taxi!' he said loudly.

'Ah, oui. Merci,' smiled Doris.

In the lavatory, she stared from the passport photo to her face in the mirror. Fantastique! There were a few alterations yet to be made, but right in front of her eyes Doris Hendy was changing into Juliette Dalmain. Her waist was still a little thick and her eyes were still brown but, as she watched, they slowly brightened to a glacier-blue.

She gave the diary a cursory look, but somehow she had already begun to assimilate everything about her new persona. She knew that she was an ambitious junior partner in a firm of solicitors in Paris; that her parents owned an hotel in Montmartre, and that Jean Paul would not last. It did not bother her that Doris was shrinking into a small corner of her mind. She was excited and calm at the same time.

As she rode in the train back to London she wondered about the real Juliette. She wondered but she did not worry. Taking out her mobile she began to speak rapidly in French.

# Man Falling off Cliff

That morning, thinking I was about to be promoted, I had bounced into the manager's office and stumbled out, jobless. Still in shock, I got home to find a note from my wife saying that she had taken the cat and gone to live with her lover. Lover? The final straw, in amongst the final demands for electricity and water rates, was a letter from the hospital asking me to come in for further tests.

Rhossili Bay is lovely in the summer but this was midwinter. The car park was deserted and the café shut. I had vague thoughts about pipes and running engines as I sat contemplating my knees. Giant waves stormed the beach below me, spewing clouds of seagulls into the sky. I'd read somewhere that drowning was almost pleasant.

The wind screamed and buffeted the car and I was half-lifted off my feet as I got out. I would hide somewhere and die quietly of hypothermia - it was painless, or so I'd heard.

The wind ripped rough fingers through what little hair I had left as I fought with the zip on my jacket. Leaning forwards into the gale, I staggered towards the cliff edge looking for a likely hollow. The best I could find was no more than a curve in the earth below an outcrop. I curled myself up, stuck my hands in my pockets and waited.

A small rock hurtled past my head followed by several others. Two legs appeared in front of my face.

'Help!'

A thin body slid past and began to disappear over the edge. A rock hit my head as I grabbed at his sleeves.

'That was close!'

He was no more than a kid. A kid in a hoody.

'What do you think you're doing?' My voice came out in an embarrassing, girly shriek.

'Ending it all.' He disappeared inside his jacket and came up with a lit cigarette. 'Till you saved me, that is.'

He took a deep drag and gave me a wink. 'Thanks mate.' He reached out to hug me and hung on as he began to slip sideways.

As I edged away he looked at me out of the corner of his eye. 'Anyway, what are you doing here?'

'Same.' I saw no reason to lie.

'Jumping?'

'Freezing.'

'Ah,' he shook his head. 'Takes hours that does. Days even. Stupid.'

'Stupid yourself,' I said. 'That wasn't much of a jump, more like a slither.'

'Lost my bottle, didn't I? Changed my mind mid-leap, like.'

'What made you ... ?' My teeth chattered in the wind.

He took another drag of his cigarette. 'No money, no job, no girlfriend.' The cigarette was tossed away into the wind. 'You?'

'Same.'

He zipped up his hoody. 'Ah well,' he said, 'I'm off. Good luck with the freezing.' I heard him whistling as he swung himself up the cliff.

I sat there for an hour, then pulled myself up and trudged back to my car. It wasn't there. I felt for my keys in my pockets but they had gone. So had my wallet.

Just then the heavens opened.

## Fast Friendly Service

'Daddy's home!' Eddie Fly, still in his dirty overalls, threw himself into a sagging armchair and tore open a can of beer. Wiping his mouth with the back of his hand he punched the buttons of the remote control until he found the channel he wanted. Without taking his eyes from the screen, he reached for the lukewarm packet of pie and chips and wolfed down the contents.

'Miss Saigon!'

Eddie loved quiz shows. He squirmed pleasurably in his seat and broke open another can, braying with derision when a man got his question wrong.

'Stupid tosser!' he jeered, spraying flakes of pastry into the air.

He balled up the empty chip packet and threw it over his shoulder. A high, thin whine drew his eyes to the sideboard as a small white dog crawled warily from underneath, blinking nervously. Its fur was dirty and matted and its black nose twitched at the smell of food.

'Come on then, Bobbykins. Come to Daddy.' Eddie cooed and held out his fingers while feeling for the can with his other hand.

The dog had been his mother's and had never liked Eddie or his games. It frantically scrabbled backwards as Eddie threw the can with vicious accuracy.

'Bull's eye!'

He bared his teeth with pure pleasure as the dog yelped, then turned his face back to the flickering television where a woman was talking about recent floods. He stared at her coldly. She was small and curvy, not his type at all. Eddie liked tall, angular women - powerful, stern women. He glanced up through the vase of grubby pink flowers to the cheap photo frame behind. His mother's face stared out disapprovingly.

A man's voice announced: 'It's five past seven, so sit up straight and mind your manners, because it's time for *Juxtaposition*!'

Eddie came alive, sitting up in his chair and furiously brushing crumbs off his chest. His mother's eyes watched him coldly and he leapt up to turn her picture to the wall. The small dog cringed as his booted feet came near and Eddie could see one small white paw. He fought down the urge to stamp on it. Plenty of time for that later.

He raced back to the chair and flung his legs out in front of him. His open mouth was a rictus of pleasure as his goddess came into view.

Nadia Fermore was assured and supercilious, in a floor length black coat and clinging catsuit in ...

' ... leather,' breathed Eddie.

Her boots had high stiletto heels that clicked as she moved around. Tall and gaunt with short black hair, gelled back severely from her face, Nadia was everything that Eddie desired. Her words were cutting as she gave instructions to the anxious contestants.

'Do you understand me?' She thundered.

'Oh, yes, yes. I do,' whispered Eddie, slouching down lower in the chair and sliding his hand inside his overalls.

He kept his eyes fixed on the icy woman and his breath came faster as he called out answers to question after question until ...

'What is the colloquial French word for werewolf?'

'Lupus!' Eddie erupted, shrieking.

'That is not the correct answer.'

As Nadia reprimanded the cowering wreck in front of her, Eddie slumped in the chair. 'I knew that.'

The severe face on the screen curled its lips in derision as it faded and was replaced by a grinning jack-o'-lantern. Children's voices chanted 'Ghosts, Ghouls and Vampires' as a man urged viewers to: 'Lock all the doors, take the phone off the hook and feed the dog. Our special Halloween's entertainment continues in a moment with *The Howling*.'

## Fast Friendly Service

'Bloody rubbish,' Eddie muttered, then jumped as something wet touched his hand. The starving dog was trying to lick his fingers. Eddie aimed a punch but it was too quick and ran back under the sideboard. He went over and turned his mother's picture around. She looked at him with dislike.

'Ah, shit.'

She'd made him promise to look after the filthy mutt, and he didn't want her coming back to haunt him, especially not tonight. Not that he believed in all that crap. Nothing frightened Eddie.

'Ghoulies, ghosties, werewolves,' he mimicked as he slouched out to the littered kitchen, grabbed himself another can and reluctantly pulled down a cheap box of dog meal from the shelf. He took out a meagre handful and spitefully scattered the pieces in amongst the wet dog mess in the corner. The dog waited until Eddie was safely back in the chair before it crept out to fall ravenously on the biscuit bits.

Eddie watched the TV and yawned in boredom as yet another woman screamed and died a bloody death. The strident ringing of the telephone was a welcome diversion.

'Edward Fly, certified plumber. How may I help you?' Eddie had read an article on customer relations and was nothing if not polite.

'Mr. Fly, I know it's a terrible imposition to ask you to come out tonight but I have urgent need of your expertise.'

The hairs on the back of Eddie's neck grew erect. It sounded like ... her! He exhaled audibly.

' ... leaking pipes. Mr. Fly ... are you there?'

Oh, baby - just keep talking, Eddie thought, as his hand strayed inside his overalls.

'Yes, madam I'm here.'

'I mean - you must be on your way to a party or some function?'

Eddie didn't have any friends to go to a party with. He didn't like anyone and nobody liked him. People used his services because he was quick and cheap, but he knew they were always relieved when he left.

He cleared his throat. 'Can I have your name and address, madam?'

## Man Falling off Cliff

The woman's voice became insulting. 'You may, Mr. Fly.'

Eddie's groin grew hotter.

'My name is Garew, Louise Garew, and I live in the old Upshott house in Northolt woods. Do you know it?'

Eddie knew it alright. His hand stilled and his mouth turned down - it was a godforsaken place and a good thirty miles away.

'You will be suitably rewarded, of course.' Her clipped voice sent delicious shivers skittering down Eddie's spine.

He looked at his watch and calculated swiftly. 'Nine o'clock alright?'

'Excellent. I'll have someone come and open the gates for you.'

Eddie raced into the kitchen - no time for a bath. He rummaged around on the shelf, found an old bottle of *Macho* aftershave and slathered it liberally around his neck. He debated whether he should change into a clean shirt but decided that she would be the sort of woman who would like him in greasy overalls. Women did like them - he'd seen plenty of them leering at him while he worked. He was hurrying out into the living room when he tripped over the unsuspecting dog.

'That's it! You've had it!' he snarled picking himself up. He tried to grab the dog but it had wriggled under the sideboard again.

'If I wasn't in a hurry, I'd do you now but there'll be plenty of time later - we'll have lots of games when Daddy comes home, won't we?'

The dog whined and Eddie grinned with sadistic pleasure. Plenty of time.

He unhooked his keys and whistling, opened the front door.

His white van stood outside with 'E. Fly - Domestic Plumber - Fast, Friendly Service' printed on the side. He tipped his head up and sniffed the air; it had stopped raining and clouds were clearing from the face of the moon. Eddie my lad, he thought, it looks as if tonight could be your night.

Something thumped into his calves, making him stumble and he saw the dog racing away down the street.

'I'll kill you, you bastard!' he screamed.

A light went on next door, but the elderly lady hastily drew the curtains when he turned and glared.

'Nosy old bitch,' Eddie said loudly and got into the van.

He drove down the dual carriageway and took the turning for Northolt. As the roads narrowed he wondered about the woman. What was she like, this Louise Garew? It sounded French. Something niggled at the back of his mind then danced away.

It could be her; Nadia Fermore could be her stage name, but if it was her - what was she doing in this neck of the woods and in the old Upshott place? The last he'd heard, it was little more than a ruin. Eddie picked his nose anxiously as he remembered her voice. Nah, he was being stupid, the woman was probably short and dumpy with five kids. The van turned a corner and the full moon cruised into view. Eddie, not one given to romantic nonsense, nevertheless stared at it and made a fervent wish.

The wooded road became unnaturally dark as Eddie drove through but he didn't notice. He played a game over and over in his mind, and the game was what he would do to the dog later. Eddie was very inventive in his particular brand of cruelty. He could already hear the wails of anguish and a smile of pleasure hovered around his mouth. The neighbours wouldn't complain - they were used to it. And besides, they were all afraid of him, bunch of useless old tossers. Eddie laughed out loud and then stopped as he heard the sputtering of the engine.

'Fuck's sake!'

The van slowed and he quickly steered it onto the grass verge. He looked at the gauges as the engine died and thumped his hands against the steering wheel.

'No petrol! You WANKER!'

He sat thinking for a moment in the silence, then reached for his tool bag and got out. He kicked the tyres in fury, then started trudging up the road.

The house couldn't be far now and he could see his way clearly in the moonlight. He strode along, whistling soundlessly and dismissed the fact that the darkness wasn't right somehow. Not right. It seemed to keep pace with him like a cloud of flies following a bad smell. There was a queer feeling of exultation emanating from the darkness. He scratched the back of his neck and started whistling the theme tune from *Juxtaposition*. He became uneasy when he heard low growling somewhere to his left, but he spat on the ground and continued walking. Nothing frightened Eddie, right?

Shuffling and shifting noises started to come from all around, and he ran his tongue over his lips, quickening his pace and glancing to either side as he went.

Sudden howling sent him spinning around.

'Jesus Christ! What the f... ?'

Eddie liked torturing little things but big dogs frightened the shit out of him. His heart galloped in his chest but there was nothing to hear, nothing, only his laboured breathing. He forced himself to relax, but then he screamed, a high girlish scream, as a cackling and chuckling came from the undergrowth to his right.

He spun around again as, from the left, a tinny, amused voice said: 'Eddie Fly! Whatcha doing, Eddie?'

He fumbled in his bag and brought out a heavy wrench and waved it wildly.

'Come on then, you bastard - where are you?'

The silence was absolute and Eddie felt for his groin, holding himself for comfort.

'Eddie, you dirty little boy - stop that right now!' The familiar voice made him moan in horror. Eddie whirled around and felt himself letting go, soaking his overalls, as his mother's disembodied face floated out from the trees. Stained lips drew back from long yellow teeth as she hissed.

The cackling started again as Eddie turned and raced clumsily up the road, his tool bag banging and clanking against his legs.

'Oh, Jesus! Oh don't - I'm sorry, I'm sorry,' he sobbed.

'Mr. Fly?'

Eddie spun around again in terror, then he stumbled in relief towards the flashlight and the cool voice.

'Is there a problem, Mr. Fly?' The light blinded him and he started gabbling.

'I heard ... things and I saw a face! My mother ... '

The flashlight swung around in an arc and Eddie's jaw dropped as he saw the floor length coat and the high heels.

'There are strange noises in these woods at night,' she said. 'But I have to admit to disappointment that an educated man like yourself would be so easily frightened.'

It was her! Eddie babbled in the presence of his goddess. 'I wasn't exactly frightened, just startled. You see, I ... '

She turned her chiselled head dismissively. 'There are your culprits,' she said, pointing.

Eddie turned and saw three children running away down the road laughing. One of them carried some sort of a mask on a pole and a large dog ran alongside. Eddie felt stupid and wished them all a painful death.

'Trick or treat, Mr. Fly?'

Eddie could have sworn she was laughing, but then she strode off, her high heels clicking, and he had to run to keep up.

Twin iron gates loomed into view.

'Would you?' she asked him haughtily and handed him a large iron key. They passed through and walked up to the dark house.

Eddie stared in disbelief. 'It's a bloody ruin!' he said.

Louise Garew stared at him. 'You really are a rude little man aren't you?' she said icily.

Eddie wilted under her glare. 'No - I didn't mean - I mean, I'm sure it's very nice inside.'

'Would you like to see?' She stared at him intently. 'Is it your wish that you come in, Mr. Fly?'

Eddie swallowed. 'Yes.'

The massive doors swung open and loud music and laughter hit him like a wave. Eddie gaped. Lights blazed everywhere and the great hall was filled with elegant people. Some of them turned to stare at him.

Eddie turned to look at her. 'But the house was in darkness,' he whispered.

She reproved him with a smiling mouth and cold eyes. 'Mr. Fly,

Have you never heard of shutters?'

Eddie looked about him anxiously as he followed her into the noisy room.

She waved an elegant hand. 'Just a small party. Do have a drink.'

Eddie felt the heat rising in his body as she slipped her coat off. Her catsuit clung to every curve - not that she had that many, he observed with satisfaction. The high heels made her thrust out her pelvis as she walked, and he watched her buttocks flex and move - high and round, like a boy's. Eddie was ecstatic.

She moved smoothly back to him and held out a frosted glass of purple liquid.

Eddie sniffed it suspiciously. 'What's in it?'

She fixed him with a stare. 'Hemlock, deadly nightshade and wolf's bane.'

Eddie giggled weakly. 'Better not have too many then.' He leered at her over his glass. 'I've got your pipes to fix.' He gulped down the drink, which was surprisingly delicious. Bubbles crisped over his tongue.

'Ah, yes,' she murmured, moving closer. 'My pipes. You must fix those for me, Eddie. But later, there's plenty of time. Plenty of time.'

Her words set off tiny alarm bells in his head, but then she put a hand to her throat and slowly drew down the zipper of her cat suit, exposing the fine bones of her chest.

'It's so warm in here, don't you think?' she asked, lifting her chin in sexual invitation.

Eddie swallowed - he had died and gone to heaven!

A crowd of people wandered over and Louise introduced them.

'Sir Ralph Hingley, Lady Sarah Whitcombe. Oh, and this is my cousin, Robert Meyers. I've thrown the party in his honour.'

The slight young man didn't shake Eddie's hand but gave him a friendly smile as he handed him another drink. 'Friend of Lou's are you?' he enquired in a pleasant manner, lounging against the wall.

Eddie crossed his fingers in the air. 'Me and Lou are like this.'

The man straightened up. 'I'm sure you are,' he murmured and walked away.

## Fast Friendly Service

Eddie frowned uneasily, but then another drink was pressed into his hand and he realized that he was probably the wittiest man alive, as people gathered around, gravely considering the statements he made and laughing uproariously at his jokes. Earlier, he had been aware of his dirty clothes and the acrid steaminess of his crotch but nobody else seemed to notice and now Eddie couldn't care less. He was euphoric. This was his world! This was where he belonged! Suddenly the room started to lurch and spin.

'Had a bit too much, old chap?' someone asked. 'Need a hair of the dog?'

A woman tittered and then the whole crowd started laughing. Eddie didn't like the sound of it; it sounded rough and spiteful and he felt sick. Where was the food? Didn't these fucking people eat?

'Get ready - it's time for *Juxtaposition*.' Louise Garew stood on a podium, long elegant fingers tapping her hips.

Everyone clapped loudly, but for once the imperious voice failed to get a reaction from Eddie. He felt himself sliding down the wall and sat with his legs splayed out, trying to focus. The glittering chandeliers blurred and merged and he closed his eyes.

His nose wrinkled as he became aware of a strong dog smell. He felt Bobbykins sniff and lick his fingers and meant to curl his hand into a fist, but found he couldn't be bothered to move. He sucked in his breath as sharp teeth grazed his knuckles then screamed in agony as the dog crunched down on his fingers.

'Come along then old man, let's help you up.' Robert Meyers and another man were pulling on his arms.

'Wha... ? Where you taking me?' Eddie slurred as they dragged him along.

'Downstairs, old chap. Don't want to miss it do you? I understand you're very good at them? *Games* I mean.'

Eddie tried to focus as his feet dragged and bumped against the stone steps. 'Where's the fuckin' food?' he snarled. 'Be alright if I have some food.'

'Yes,' said Robert. 'I know exactly how you feel.'

They entered a small underground chamber to a round of applause.

Eddie opened bleary eyes and saw the audience seated in rows along the back.

Louise Garew stood in the centre of a small stage under a banner that read *Juxtaposition*. Eddie sagged between the two men as she began reading out the rules.

'Always wan ... wannit to be in iss show.' He smiled dreamily up at Robert.

'And now you are, Eddie.'

At the back of the stage was a circular device with hooks. Eddie, unresisting, was stripped of his clothing, lifted up and put into place. It was pleasantly comfortable as he swayed around gently and blinked sleepily at his goddess.

Louise finished speaking and the audience leaned forward attentively as a young woman came forward and drew lines and numbers in red ink all over Eddie's body. The audience sighed. He tried to focus and saw several large dogs in amongst the people. They don't fucking care what they do, these aristocrats, he thought, trying not to laugh. They just don't fucking care.

'What is the name of the Romanian count who supposedly drank the blood of his victims?'

'Vlad the Impaler,' giggled Eddie.

'Vlad the Impaler!' someone shouted.

'Correct - you have number five.' The audience buzzed.

'What 'M' is the latin for mother?'

'Mater.' Eddie shuddered.

Someone repeated the word and was awarded another number.

'Oy,' Eddie tried to shout. 'Oy, wha' bout me?'

The questions went on and Eddie got bored. His eyes began to droop. Suddenly a sharp stinging in his chest made him yelp, and he looked down to see four long, deep cuts beginning to well blood. As the hot liquid poured down and slowly obliterated the number six on his stomach, Eddie giggled uneasily.

Louise Garew stood in front of him and smiled. Eddie squinted. There was something wrong with her face. She looked ...

'This one is for you, Eddie,' she said, baring her long teeth. 'What is the colloquial French word for werewolf?'

Eddie knew the answer. He knew it. He also knew that the tiny screaming voice at the back of his mind was right - that to answer meant death. He looked directly into her queer, yellow eyes.

'Loup-garou,' he whispered.

There was a deathly silence. Then they fell on him, howling and tearing, sucking and pulling. His screaming went on for a long time before it stopped and then the only sound in the bare room was the cracking of bones and methodical slurping.

'Happy darling?' Louise looked deep into Robert's eyes as she licked the fur around his mouth.

'Mmm, and very, very full.' He patted his stomach ruefully, belched and growled in mock play as she nuzzled his neck.

'I saved you the best part.'

'I noticed.' He turned to look behind him. 'Not much left.'

'Only the eyes,' she said. 'Nobody wanted the eyes.'

He stood up and stretched.

'Do you have to go?'

'People to see, Lou,' he said, and smiled as he kissed her. 'Things to do.'

The van was waiting as they walked outside. She leaned up to kiss him.

'Until next year, darling.'

The van disappeared down the road, fresh with maroon paint and black and gold lettering that read: 'R. Meyers. Vermin Control. Satisfaction Guaranteed.'

# Biddy

On one of those high summer days conjured up for the very young, a large tabby cat sagged over the windowsill of an end-of-terrace house. From his position above the sloping front garden his yellow eyes regarded the country road that meandered past the gate and undulated upward to the dark mystery of Bluebell Wood in the hazy distance.

The cat blinked at a cloud of insects alighting on sprawling Sweet Williams, swarming high over multicoloured hollyhocks and falling drunkenly into the tangled hedge of thick honeysuckle. His eyes narrowed into slits against the shimmering, dancing light and he dropped onto the path and padded around the corner of the house to where it was cool and damp. Threading his way through a patch of cabbages, he flopped down in the shade of an elderly gooseberry bush. All was quiet except for faint voices of children playing down the road and the drone of bees around the lavender. Presently, his whiskers began to twitch as he slept.

The shadow of the chimney had lengthened and moved over the rooftop, when a sharp noise disturbed him. He lifted his head to see a woman striding down the path, away from the chicken shed. One empty sleeve flapped and her greasy hair, cut severely short, was jammed to one side with a clip. She held a squawking, flailing bird by the feet. Pausing at the side of the steps, she clamped the bird under her left arm and, using the knife in her good hand, bent to her task. Her wrist twisted and the squawking became more frantic, more liquid then it stopped. The tabby rolled over and played with a dead beetle. He heard the woman's heavy, booted feet on the steps, and the rattling of the latch on the outhouse door. The iron tap

## Biddy

screeched and water gushed, then the kitchen door slammed and all was quiet again.

A child of about five years of age, wearing a thin cotton frock, ran panting up the hill towards the house. Her face and limbs were dirty from play and she crossed her legs as she pressed down on the stiff catch of the gate. It groaned open and she glanced up at the bedroom window next door. As if on cue, the lace curtains twitched. Stepping through, she carefully checked that the latch was down - her aunt was most particular about this, and it didn't do to anger her aunt.

At the top of the path two giant columns, bearing the scuffmarks of small feet scrabbling to catch a glimpse of Swansea Bay in the distance, stood guard over the front door. Clamping a hand between her legs the girl ran around the side of the house and the cat got to its feet, swaying against the bush, his tail an erect welcome. The girl ran past her grandmother's kitchen window and came skidding to a halt in front of the lavatory door.

Her eyes widened with horror and her mouth fell open for several heartbeats - 'catching flies', her aunt called it. The thing in front of her dangled and fluttered on the handle making the head bounce sickeningly. Its feet, bound round and round with saved string, curled, flexed and clutched at the air. She registered three long, grey pinfeathers on its right wing and shoved her fist into her mouth. A blister of blood formed in the gaping beak and burst, draining into the dark, congealing pool on the flagstones. One half-closed eye accused her and angry voices began a tirade in her head.

'*Have to have stitches you will - I could put my fist in that hole. You've ruined those socks.*'

'*Black blood in the baby's mouth, Winnie. Push harder.*'

'*Just some rags soaking - get away from there now!*' ... '*But the water's red, Mammy.*' ... '*Mind your own business!*'

She looked down as a splash of red spotted her sandal and felt a sudden release, soaking and hot down her legs.

'Granny!' she screamed. 'Biddy's bleeding to death!'

The kitchen door banged open and her aunt clattered out.

'What is it? What's the matter? Stop that silly nonsense right now!'

The child sobbed and pulled at her aunt's overall. 'Do something!'

The woman slapped away the small hand. 'It's dead, can't you see? Oh, ych a fi! Look at the stinking mess you've made, you mochyn!' She grabbed the child with one strong hand and shook the other one in her face. The girl looked at the exposed half-arm with the four small pink blobs that should have been fingers, and screamed even louder.

'Edie! Leave her alone!' Tall and gaunt, the child's grandmother came out of the house, wiping her hands on her apron. Her long skirt swept the floor as she walked over to the sobbing child and drew the hot face against her hip. She glanced at the chicken.

'Why didn't you do this earlier, Edie? You knew full well that she would be home for her tea. It was her favourite bird too.' The muffled sobs increased in intensity and the old woman tenderly smoothed the child's tangled hair; but her eyes were uncharacteristically hard on the defiant face of her eldest daughter. 'You can be a nasty piece of work sometimes, d'you know that?'

The child peeped out from her grandmother's skirt with one, round eye and saw her aunt's lips whiten.

'She has to know, Mama. She has to learn.' The aunt put a foot on the steps and viciously laced up her boots with the calloused fingers of one hand. 'You and that sister of mine have filled her head with dreams and fairytales - she even thinks that that mangy tom enjoys being kissed and dressed up in doll's clothes. You all make her think that the world is lovely when it's not and the sooner she wakes up to that fact the easier it will be on her.'

The grandmother put her hands over the child's ears. 'She's just a baby, Edie, and her father ... '

'Is dead these past two years.' The aunt threw her head back, snorting derision. 'Someone has to show her how hard life is. How does she think food gets on the table? Who does she think puts it there?' She jerked tight the string of her overalls and jabbed her thumb to her chest. 'Muggins, that's who!'

'Winnie does her best ... '

## Biddy

The aunt snorted. 'Oh yes, let's hear it for Saint Winifred!'

'She's doing her best, Edie - two jobs isn't easy when ... '

'I had a bloody good job in Gloucester! I had prospects!'

The child watched the wide-open mouth and saw a stream of spittle disappearing into the deep crevice at the side of her Aunt's mouth.

As her grandmother sniffed sharply the child burrowed deeper into the meaty smells of gravy and roasting potatoes and waited.

'You didn't have to come home.'

'Oh please, Mama! After that God-awful letter about duty?'

'And haven't you just loved rubbing our noses in that great sacrifice ever since?'

The words were softly spoken but the child screwed up her eyes as her aunt's good hand closed into a fist. It seemed to her that hours passed as the two women, chests heaving, glared at one another; then the girl looked up at her aunt and saw her swallow. Grabbing a shovel, the woman stomped back up the steps, aiming a vicious kick at the cat who melted into a row of runner beans.

'Granny,' the child whimpered. 'Will Aunt Edie murder me?'

'Oh, my heavens!' The grandmother took a rag out of her pocket. 'Blow your nose now, there's a good girl.'

'She's always saying she will and she made Biddy bleed to death.'

'No, no my dear, Biddy died before you came home. She wanted to go to visit Jesus in heaven, see? And so she asked Aunt Edie to help her along, that's all. Come on now, come in and we'll get you cleaned up.'

The child looked back at the bird, still now, with its white wings fallen open. It looked like an angel.

That evening, kneeling in her nightdress by the grate, the girl crunched noisily on a thick piece of toasted bread as she counted the newly hatched chicks that had been incubating in an old woollen cardigan in a box against the fender - four brown, three toffee-mottled and one yellow. Lifting the chick to her face she gently riffled the yellow fluff with her nose and the chick peeped loudly.

'Look, Granny! It's Biddy come back!'

Her grandmother put down her darning, leaned back in the rocking chair and smiled. 'That's right, my dear, that's right.'

The aunt, sitting at the scrubbed table, rattled her newspaper in annoyance, but held her tongue.

In a dark corner of the kitchen the grandfather clock ticked away the hours and underneath, curled up in a battered doll's pram, the tabby cat's whiskers twitched as he slept.

## Promontory

Percy sat on his promontory and stared out to sea. His eyes were bleak and grey as he scanned the horizon. Clickety, click, click went the knitting needles while the ball of clear blue wool tumbled softly and unwound.

There were no other penguins on the rock; Percy's violent rages saw to that. All the other birds clustered in the distance and stared at him moodily. His skill with wool and needles was widespread and sought after, but never would he agree to knit for another penguin.

Plash! A small silver sardine flopped onto a rock below and turned to look up at Percy with bulging eyes.

'Do you have that which I desire?' it gasped, affecting a smile.

Clickety, click. 'I might,' said Percy, laying his needles down and eyeing the plump little body with distaste. 'But I will have to come down and measure you for I fear you may have gained some weight since last we met.'

Taking his wickerwork basket in his beak, Percy jumped and slid down to the sardine.

The fish gazed at him expectantly. 'It is all the colours of the rainbow?'

Percy opened the lid of the basket and took out a sleeveless jumper of raspberry, teal, sky blue and lemon.

'Oh!' gasped the fish. 'So beautiful!' His eyes watered as he appealed to Percy. 'Quickly, help me to put it on.'

Percy squeezed and tugged the miraculous garment over the sardine's head. It stuck at the chest, but with Percy heaving and the fish gyrating, the jumper was finally in place.

'Oh, yes!' said the fish. 'It feels marvellous. How do I look?

Honestly now, do not flatter me.'

'Honestly?' said Percy, taking a long breath in through his nose. 'You look fat and ridiculous.' And with that, he stuffed the creature into his basket, slamming the lid shut.

Percy sat on his promontory, his eyes fixed on the ship in the distance. Clickety click. The crimson garment grew rapidly as his needles flew and glittered in the pale sunshine. He was out of sorts. His last meal had been four days ago, and that had been a scrawny, diseased mackerel. Of course, he could have eaten any one of the twenty or so plump fish, still writhing and crying in the plastic container concealed in his basket, but that was not his way. Not for Percy the surge of life-giving energy that came with eating a healthy fish. No. He only allowed himself the occasional corpse - the ones that were freshly dead or did not have long to live.

As the ship came closer to land, Percy deftly cast off the beautiful garment and popped it in the basket. He waited.

'Am I too late? Oh, please do not tell me that it is so.' An emaciated salmon lay on the shore, its eyes dull and eaten away.

Percy picked up his basket and hopped quickly down to the water. 'No, no,' he soothed, 'I have it here.'

'Oh, praise be,' sighed the fish and lay back exhausted.

Percy was mercifully quick as he bit off the salmon's head and crunched stolidly at the bones. He bowed his head. Dear God, how much longer?

Ten winters ago, when the ship had first come, Bella had struggled to alert everyone to the dangers, but no one would listen. Enthralled by the shiny metal and hypnotic smells, they clamoured around and the men had thrown food. Then it was noticed that certain seals and penguins had begun to disappear. After a while some of these managed to return, but they were deformed, *queer*, and people avoided them. But still everyone gathered around the ship.

Bella alone spoke up. 'Come away,' she cried. 'Come away!'

'Hush, Bella,' Percy had whispered nervously. 'Everyone is

looking.'

But Bella had pushed him off and ran up and down the beach giving warning to anyone who would listen. For hours she called, the light glancing off her intricately patterned yellow jumper while Percy clung to the shadows, watching.

Eventually, fearing her voice, the fat fish had delivered her to the scientists. She had been stripped naked, caged and put out to starve on the ice.

'See?' said the fat fish triumphantly. 'See what happens when you swim against the tide.'

He could have saved her. Somehow he could have. But no, deep inside, in a dark and shameful place, he knew he was glad that it was she and not he out there. So he'd climbed up to the promontory and watched, because that's what he did best, didn't he? The sleek, well-fed survivor that was Percy watched, day after day, while Bella's shrieks turned to whimpers and eventual silence. And then all the fat fish had come to the surface and cheered as the men took her body away.

'You there - penguin!' Booted feet crunched up the shingle and a grimy face peered down at him. 'Jeez! You've got to be the scrawniest bird I've ever seen!' The man poked Percy's breastbone that jutted out like the prow of a boat. Percy turned away, disinterested.

'You have them?'

Percy nodded and kicked the basket.

'How many?' The man flung open the lid of the container and the fat fish broiled away from his bloodstained hands, flashing their multi-coloured jumpers and screaming out protests of innocence.

'Nice bit of knitting, Perce, but there's not enough of them I'm afraid. Your contract states forty.'

Percy grimaced blearily and shrugged.

The man thoughtfully scraped his fingers over his chin. There was a moment when Percy could have screamed, but then he really couldn't be bothered as the man threw him into the basket and slammed the lid shut.

## Man Falling off Cliff

Percy sat on his promontory. Click, clickle, click. Two hundred other penguins surrounded him but he had long ago ceased to be unnerved by their constant chattering. Now their proximity and warmth soothed him. His feet tingled and he moved them carefully, feeling the precious weight rock against him. Putting aside his knitting for a moment, he bent down to tenderly rotate the egg that nestled under his down feathers.

His newly fashioned cloaca felt hot and torn, but he hardly noticed. All the love in his heart was directed towards this, his unborn child and he loved her, (he knew it would be a girl), with all the fierce, pent-up passion he had never shown to Bella.

The other mothers pressed softly against him and preened in their beautiful knitted garments of delicate lilacs, peaches and pinks.

Percy watched the ship fade to a dot on the horizon. It would be another five years before they came back so there was time enough. He picked up the needles and began to fashion a tiny, intricately patterned yellow garment. Time enough for them all.

## TIGER LILY FLAMES

On the first Monday of each month, I treat myself by coming here to Llwyn Hall to have afternoon tea. The two young men who own the place make such a fuss of me, bringing me scones and jam or tiny ham sandwiches on delicate china plates. Mostly, I like to eat outside where I can see all the trees and flowers, but if the weather is bad I'll sit indoors in the oak-panelled sitting room by the open fire and think how different it all would have been if Alfred was here.

During one of these bad-weather days, one of the young men will come over and chat and ask me how I'm doing and I always say, 'couldn't be better.' They're sensitive enough not to stare at my arthritic old hands as I sip my tea. We're on first name terms now and I know all about their plans for extending the hall and gardens, but I was pleased to learn that they will leave the rhododendron garden as it is.

When I've finished my tea I'll make my way around to the garden, where I'll sit on the stone bench and just breathe in the colours. It's completely private there and the staff leave me alone with my memories.

Ten years now I've been coming here to sit by the rhododendrons, and can clearly remember the day they were planted; the deep holes and the careful, loving way they were pressed in. Pink, scarlet, white, lilac and orange - I love them all; but if I were forced to pick a favourite it would have to be the orange, with its hot, tiger lily flames. Alfred hated orange - too exotic, too carefree and out of control. He hated wild birds too.

I always save some bread to crumble and scatter around. I know that within ten minutes, sparrows, robins and finches will come to feed and if I sit perfectly still, they will not mind me. One year, there was even a seagull but it had a wicked beak and mean little eyes and frightened all the other birds away.

It sounds foolish I know, but on Alfred's birthday, I bring my photograph album and talk to him about my holidays in Brighton, parties at the club and my good friend, Jim.

My house is not far from here - just up the hill and off the main road. It's quiet and I have a little garden. There isn't room for much in the way of plants, but it's manageable and I put in what colour I can. Ten years ago, just before Alfred disappeared, I'd scraped together a bit of money to buy a small rhododendron. It was a dwarf and wouldn't have grown very big. So pretty. I'd planted it carefully and gone inside to fetch some water when Alfred came in through the back door.

'What have you done now?' he asked and went to look.

I heard banging and rushed to the window. He had taken the shovel and was slicing and hacking at the little bush. His face was a deep blood red.

They say that rage gives you the strength of ten men. I can vouch for that. The wheelbarrow was as light as a feather that night as I danced down the road to Llwyn Hall. I curled Alfred's body artistically around the deep roots of a rhododendron and shovelled mounds of earth on top, and my heart was lighter than it had been in years as I jumped up and down to firm the soil.

Five days later, the police asked. 'Does he have a lady friend?'

I wept as the neighbours clucked sympathetically and squirrelled the gossip away as fodder for the winter.

It's getting colder so I won't stay too much longer. Such lovely flowers - but that orange in particular is glorious.

## Away with the Fairies

Michael O'Leary was coming apart at the seams. He sat in his car, trying to balance files and sheets of paper on his knees. Rainwater sluiced over the windows as cars sped past, their lights turning the windscreen into a coloured waterfall. He rubbed a shaking hand over his face and glanced at his watch. Christ! Four o'clock and he still had three more to see before he could finish.

He squeezed his eyes shut and wished himself home in his flat, empty now with no one there to give him grief; though there would be the usual pile of bills and final demands on the mat. His knuckles turned white as he gripped the steering wheel; he must be mad to keep doing this job. He'd loved it at first, even though the wages were lousy, but they kept piling on the work as though he was some sort of robot and all the joy had gone. Now all he wanted to do was go home, get into bed with the covers over his head and never come out again.

A few more cars splashed past. 'All coming home from your neat little offices with your neat little salaries,' he snarled.

He knew he was acting irrationally, but couldn't stop himself waving with manic bonhomie at the next car. 'Bet you've got a neat little secretary too, haven't you?' he yelled and his wave turned into a vicious V sign.

He sat back in shock. Shit! Get a hold! What the hell was happening to him?

He bent his head to the files and started chewing the stubs of his nails. The loose pile of papers slid gracefully off his knees and lay scattered on the floor of the car.

'Look!' he screeched. 'Look at all this crap! How the hell am I supposed to manage?'

Who are you talking to, Michael? The thought made him laugh and he was frightened to find that he couldn't stop.

'Calm down now,' he muttered, wiping sweat from his upper lip. 'Calm down boy, or they'll be putting you in the loony bin.' He forced down another wave of hysteria and started the car.

Two hours later, he stood in the rain looking up at the last house. Julia would be alright, she was a bit wearing and as dotty as confetti but unlike the others she didn't have a mean bone in her body.

The door was flung open. 'Michael! Darling! How absolutely wonderful that you could make it! Come in, come in! I have been bereft! Bereft! You haven't called, you haven't rung! There's someone else, isn't there?'

Julia Rees, all of eighty and decked out in swirling magenta and yellow, was swooning with excitement.

'Come and see, darling! The pipes have sprung a leak and there's water everywhere! It's too thrilling! Where have you been you naughty boy? I thought I'd never see that angelic face again! I have been inconsolable!'

Michael scraped the wet hair off his face. 'Julia, I was here last Tuesday.'

Julia looked puzzled. 'Were you, darling?' She started waltzing around the room, waving a long chiffon scarf. 'But I've missed you so! And it's been ages! Have you eaten? I've been baking, would you believe! A Victoria sandwich - just for you!'

She bounced over to the table and came back with an exquisite bone china plate containing a jam sandwich, cut into triangles and curling delicately at the edges. 'Baking all day! My darling, I'm exhausted!' She put a hand to her forehead and floated gracefully into a chair.

'Julia, do you have a towel?' Michael had begun to shiver.

She looked at him in horror. 'Oh, but darling you're soaked! Come, come and warm yourself by the fire.' With surprising strength, she dragged him to a sagging armchair.

'Julia, it isn't on ... ' but she had bounded out of the room. He sighed and set about lighting the gas fire.

She came back with a dripping wet towel and he closed his eyes in irritation.

'Well, I'm sorry darling - they've all been used up.' She looked contrite.

'It doesn't matter, don't worry.'

He reared back as she started to towel his hair vigorously with her scarf. Normally, he would have stopped her, but today, he wasn't normal, and as the fire warmed him, he began to enjoy and be comforted by her ministrations.

'This is rather a sacred moment, don't you think Michael?' she whispered. 'Like Mary Magdalene and Our Dear Lord!'

Michael choked and began to laugh. He laughed until he was almost sick and all the while she was busily going over his hair with the wisps of chiffon.

She paused for a moment and looked at him gravely. 'Michael darling - are you taking your medication?'

'You're pinching my line, Julia!' he hiccupped. The gas fire popped and he gave a shuddering sigh. 'It's been one hell of a day, that's all.'

'Yes, darling, but what I want to know is - while you're so busy taking care of other people - who is taking care of you?'

Michael looked into the wrinkled blue eyes and saw concern and kindness there. He swallowed and stood up. 'Right then, Julia; let's have a look at these leaking pipes.'

Julia clapped happily and led the way down into her kitchen. Leak? The kitchen steamed and the floor was underneath a good twelve inches of water. More hot water flowed down the pipes in the corner.

'Voila! My flotation tank! I've put in fifteen boxes of Epsom Salts - it should be just about right now.'

He looked at the gently undulating pool in horror. 'Have you rung a plumber?'

'Darling, I've rung thousands, thousands! All I get are those horrible answering thingies.'

'Did you ask Cyril, next door?'

'Oh, I tried darling but he won't talk to me after that last business. Lord knows I've tried being patient with him, but he insists on being old! Life's too, too short don't you think?'

Michael's head ached. He didn't know where to start.

'Right then darling, are you ready? I promise you; this is just what you need.'

Julia discarded her clothing with amazing swiftness. She stepped down into the water, and her long white plait swayed gently as her skinny body disappeared into the steam.

An hour later, Michael answered the door.

'Yes?'

Four plumbers stood outside, arguing. They stopped when they saw him, then the one with thick pebble glasses stepped forward.

'Look here - PAL! We've all been called out by the same person,' he consulted a bit of paper. 'Ms. Julia Rees. And I'm telling you, this will cost you triple time - for all of us.'

He looked around smugly for approval but the others were gaping at Michael who stood framed by the light in a full-length, emerald-green satin Chinese robe.

'Are we addressing Ms. Julia Rees, perhaps?' sneered one of the others, digging his mate in the ribs.

'I'm Ms. Rees' CPN,' said Michael.

'That's Cut Price Nancy to you lot,' said the joker in a loud whisper.

They all grinned, watching for Michael's reaction.

'I'm a nurse, actually,' said Michael, smiling pleasantly.

'Marvellous what you can get on the National Health isn't it, lads?' The men guffawed loudly.

Four hours earlier, Michael would have snapped and snapped badly, but the surreal image of himself and Julia, floating dreamily around her kitchen floor made him grin. He drew himself up to his full six feet and placed one languid hand on his hip.

'Come on in boys; I'll take all four of you,' he drawled, pouting and batting his eyelashes at the suddenly uneasy plumbers. He felt okay, more than okay.

As the men scrambled back down the path, he threw back his head and laughed.

'Life's too, too short my darlings don't you think?' he called after them.

And then he went back in - to Julia.

## Double Double

Jean hung the last towel on the line and, picking up a cushion, wandered down to the bottom of the garden. Her dogs panted at her heels, flopping down at her side as she lay down on the old bench. It was cool in the shade of the apple tree and she idly opened her fingers to watch the sun's rays flicker through the branches. The scent of honey and almonds from the hedge of May blossom drifted across her face mingling with the sharp smell of wild plants in the woods beyond. She waved a fly away, smiling as she listened to the gritty noise of a fork hitting the earth in the garden next door.

'Bareee!'

Jean lifted her head and shaded her eyes to see her elderly neighbour waving a teacloth at her middle-aged son from her kitchen door. Combat trousers viciously belted beneath the bulge of his belly, he continued to dig, and every movement of the fork was punctuated with a low grunt.

'Bareee!' Her voice was high and sweet, like a bird.

The noise of the digging stopped. 'What is it now, Mother?'

'I've made us some lunch.'

'I'll just finish this patch.'

Her voice was hesitant. 'It'll get cold dear.'

Jean heard his heavy sigh and the sound of retreating footsteps. She let her head fall back and watched the flash of sunlight through her closed lids.

Edna and Barry had moved next door to Jean just over a year ago and the blue Fiesta was a familiar sight as Barry ferried his mother to the village shop or into town. Jean had never heard him complain, but recently Edna had confided that Barry had developed a bit of a temper.

'I blame those blood pressure tablets, dear,' she'd said over the dividing fence. 'Every night I pray that he'll slim down and find someone nice to marry, but at the moment I'm afraid that no decent woman will look at him ... ' Her bright eyes had seemed to fix on Jean's as she'd emphasised *decent*. 'The doctor says that he must lose weight and goodness knows that I try, but ... ' she looked around nervously and whispered. 'He's been so difficult lately and he won't touch salad you know.'

Jean thought about the rows of lettuce that Barry had planted, as she began to doze off. Edna was such a dear lady and devoted to her only son, but how much better for everybody if she had friends of her own age around her. One of the dogs began to whine and twitch in its sleep. What I wouldn't give to be a fly on the wall, Jean thought.

The bluebottle rose from the sleeping woman's face and flew towards the delicious smells coming from the house next door. It dallied over a rotting bird carcass for a few minutes and crawled over a pile of steaming dog excrement before flying in through the half-opened window. Two plates abandoned on the draining board were given immediate attention. The fly skimmed and crawled over the few leftover chips and skated across the buttery remains of sweetcorn. It paused to clean glutinous gravy from its head before vomiting over and sucking up the greasy grey morsels clinging to the bones of one of the pork chops. It ignored the small bowl of lettuce and crawled inside a glass to suck up a bead of cola from the side before flying onto the white tablecloth.

On the table were two dishes containing treacle tart and double, double whipped cream. One dish was half-eaten, the other not touched at all. In the middle of the table was a brochure for an old people's home together with the ripped up remains of a Valentine card. Had the fly been able to read, it would have picked out a word here and there - 'better off ... soon ... we ... ' One of the fragments contained a single 'J'.

Such sweetness! In a delirium out of all insect proportions, the fly sick-sucked at the cream and almost missed the warning down-rush of air. The fish slice struck the table just as it rose, zigzagging erratically across the room.

The old woman breathed heavily as she followed the fly around the kitchen. Slash! Crack! The cupboards, the sink, the cooker, the window - all bore clumps of grease from the fish slice. In panic the fly retreated to the darkness of the floor where it skittered over the half open eyes of the man before faltering and falling onto its back, buzzing and spinning into the dust in the corner.

Jean's eyes flew open and she exhaled shakily. Dear God, what a dream. Her heart was hammering and her head thumped. Her own silly fault - they were always going on about too much sun weren't they? Her throat was so dry. That tart that Edna had given her to taste earlier was probably to blame. It had been horribly sweet and the cream had been off. It was only the thought of being alone with Barry that evening that had allowed her to swallow most of it and smile her compliments. While Edna's back was turned she had surreptitiously fed the remaining morsels to her drooling pets. Getting to her feet she stumbled against one of the dogs and frowned - what was wrong with them? They weren't moving. She was leaning towards one of the still forms when the pain punched through her stomach. Doubling up and gasping for air, she fell to her knees.

A sweet voice trilled out from the top of the path. 'Jean? Are you there Jean?'

'Help me!' Jean's words came out as a mere rattle of air.

A shadow blocked out the sun. 'That'll be the Belladonna, dear. It kills the voice. I had to give Barry a triple dose.'

With her suddenly multi-faceted vision, Jean looked up to see a hundred Ednas, each holding a fish slice, each rotating gently in the rapidly darkening light.

## Stones of Tomorrow

The pebble glowed dull red in the morning light. Madeleine picked it up, feeling the vibration and energy of the ocean in her hand. Her daughter was a small, solitary figure on the beach; head bent, searching amongst the washed up flotsam along the cove.

For a moment Madeleine held the hard warmth of the stone against her face and closed her eyes. She was used to Caro's periods of endless screaming, but the recent long silences were something that had become unbearable.

She set down the stone in exactly the same spot on her daughter's windowsill and, after wiping the paintwork with a damp cloth, replaced the twisted driftwood and lines of shells with the same precision. Glancing at her watch she ran downstairs. She had given up trying to work out how her child knew the exact time, but every day at exactly eleven o'clock Caro would walk through the door and sit at the table for her milk and biscuits.

Caro placed a round, grey pebble on the kitchen table and, gazing at something over her mother's shoulder, reached for her milk. Her blond hair had been blown across her face and Madeleine put out a hand but her fingers faltered in midair. She picked up her cup instead, feeling the hot tea scald her lips.

'That's pretty,' she said.

Caro replaced the glass and moved the stone an inch to the left. Her index finger started to tap it rapidly.

'Sorrow.' The girl's voice was a flat monotone. 'Sorrow is one,' she said, breaking a biscuit in half.

'But you have two now.' Madeleine's eyes traced the fragile bones of her daughter's face and the frayed dungarees. 'Two is for joy.' She smiled brightly.

Caro looked through her. She broke the biscuit half into quarters and nibbled slowly. 'Two for tomorrow,' she said.

Madeleine looked down at her hands, tracing the thin white line where her wedding band had been. She remembered the frantic search through the house and along the beach. Her fingers rubbed away a sudden chill at the nape of her neck.

Madeleine watched as Caro, with an expressionless face, sat in terrible stillness on the floor of the studio. She had been like this for over two hours.

'Where are you, baby?'

Rain battered the window and faint calls of gulls came up from the beach. Inside, the silence was unnerving and Madeleine, wiping her hands on a cloth, got up from her easel. The commission was not going well, and the half-formed face of a local dignitary seemed to leer at her. She walked over to Geoff's canvases, stacked against the far wall. His paintings crackled with brilliant imagery - startling landscapes with giant shells and strange sea-creatures. He had just started to make a name for himself.

'Caro?'

She sighed and massaged the small of her back as she wandered over to the window. Through the rain she could just make out a mist beginning to form on the incoming tide. Suddenly he was there, at the water's edge, laughing and pointing to something in his hand. Tall and thin, with long red hair tied back in a pony tail and wearing that ridiculous checked shirt that was forever hanging out of his jeans. Curls of hair blew across his forehead and he was ...

'Sorrow is one.' Caro was standing by her side. When Madeleine looked back, Geoff had gone.

She knelt down. 'You miss Daddy, Caro?'

The girl pulled the oily cloth from her mother's hand, smoothing it against her nose and face. A sudden longing to sweep her daughter into her arms and breathe in her sweetness was overwhelming.

Instead she went to run a bath, the start of another lengthy bedtime ritual that contained the few brief intimacies that Caro allowed.

The following morning, she joined Caro on the beach. As the girl followed lines of debris, Madeleine stood and looked back at the house with purple and green hills above. The small road meandered into the village, while a few summer cottages clustered in the distance. A sudden wind blew in off the sea, pushing her hair into her face and she brushed it away absent-mindedly. Amongst the smell of seaweed and rotting crabs was something else, something familiar. She looked at the shirt cuff flapping at her wrist. Geoff's shirt. She must have put it on that morning but couldn't remember doing it. She hugged herself for warmth, feeling her ribs through the checked cloth. She hurried after Caro.

'Look, darling,' she said, picking up a whelk shell. 'It's just like the ones I used to collect when I was a little girl. You put it to your ear and you can hear the sea.'

Caro kept walking and Madeleine, hearing the waves breaking just a hundred metres from them, felt surplus and stupid. Seagulls wheeled and screamed overhead as she let the shell fall. Suddenly she felt more desolate and alone than she had been in her whole life. Worse even than when …

Caro moved on with Madeleine trailing some way behind her. Suddenly, she turned, taking Madeleine by surprise. Running past with her familiar, tiptoeing gait, she searched for, and found the abandoned shell. She began tracing the ridges and whorls with her fingers before drawing it lightly across her lips, again and again. She explored the treasure for a full five minutes before she came back and then, looking away into the distance, took hold of Madeleine's fingers and placed the shell in her hand.

Madeleine's breath caught in her throat. To any other mother, it would have been charming gift, nothing more. There had been no smile, no warmth in the giving but to Madeleine it was pure, exquisite joy.

Back at the house she watched as Caro placed a third pebble beside the other two on her windowsill. Grey and shot through with white, it seemed to fascinate as she traced the criss-cross lines with her finger.

'Three for?' Madeleine frowned, shading her eyes against the shifting light on the sea. Was that a boy on the beach? The summer cottages were still locked up and people rarely came to this secluded cove in winter. She turned to watch Caro and when she turned back the figure had gone.

'Friends,' said Caro abruptly.

'Three for a letter,' Madeleine corrected and absently stroked the silky hair on her child's head. Her hand stilled at her mistake and she waited for the terrible wailing to begin. But Caro, smoothing the pebble against her mouth, seemed preoccupied with something on the shore.

Amongst the circulars and bills the following morning was a letter. It was addressed to Geoff.

*Dear Mr. Holden*, she read. *Further to your enquiries about a placement for your daughter at Greenhaven School, we are pleased to inform you that a vacancy has now occurred and we could take Caro on the 9th September. If you would care to ring us on the telephone number below, we will forward all the necessary details.'*

They had talked about it but it seemed like years ago now. Geoff had gone to the school to check it out and had come back with a glowing report.

'The kids, Maddy, the kids!' he had said. 'The place was terrific and the teachers were really enthusiastic, but the kids! They were like Caro, a lot of them. But they seemed so ... alive!'

They had looked at their daughter, mutely rocking back and fore on the mat. Madeleine had tried to get excited at the thought of sending their only child away to live with total strangers.

'She'd come home at weekends,' he had said, stroking her arm. 'And she'd be with us every holiday.'

Yes, they'd talked about it, or rather, Geoff had while she'd listened in silence, but then suddenly Geoff couldn't seem to do the work on their small sea cottage any more. Cancer was a word they avoided but then one night, in one split-second, hand-holding moment, he was gone.

Madeleine stuffed the letter in the back of the kitchen drawer.

That night he came to her. He held her in his arms and kissed her mouth, her breasts, her stomach. His weight was sweet on her and her body responded with a spasm of release. She heard moaning that was not hers and started up in bed with her nightshirt clinging to her. Caro was wailing in the other room and Madeleine could hear the familiar, drumming sound of her head banging against the wall. Part of her felt guilt at relishing the one time that she could hold her daughter in her arms without making the situation any worse.

Ignoring the punches and biting, she walked to the windowsill and pointed out the line of pebbles and shells. Gradually Caro relaxed, sliding out of her mother's arms and touch-tapping the round stones.

'One for sorrow,' Madeleine repeated the familiar verse. 'Two for joy, three for a letter … ' she stopped abruptly.

Caro touched the fourth stone. 'Friend.'

'Four for a boy,' Madeleine said automatically, feeling ice lick down her spine.

The councillor now sported a quirky half-smile that was nothing like the dour photograph in front of her. Madeleine sighed with satisfaction. She filled the kettle for a celebratory cup of tea and it was then that she saw the boy again. Wearing cut-off jeans, he was down at the tidemark just a few yards from her daughter, intent on his own investigation.

Two years ago, a young family had made friendly advances to Caro on the beach. The disgust and fear on the mother's face would stay with her forever.

The boy's shirt tails flapped in the breeze and he was poking about with a stick in a line of seaweed. Anxiety choked her as he picked up something and took it over to Caro.

Madeleine raced down the steps and stumbled in the soft sand. Just then she saw the boy touch her daughter's arm. She held her breath and prayed that she could get to them in time, but her feet slowed and stopped as Caro put her hand out and accepted the boy's gift.

'Caro needs more than us, Maddy,' Geoff's words came back to her.

Madeleine slumped down on the sand. After a while the boy turned and walked away and Caro ran up to the house, passing her mother without a word. The white pebble was held out delicately as though it was the most precious thing in the world.

'Friend.'

The fifth pebble lay glittering in the light of the dying sun. Madeleine tumbled potatoes into the sink and held her hands under the water, staring into the distance. The beach was deserted.

Her shell lay on the counter, a small token of hope.

'Five for silver, Caro,' she said. She jumped at the piercing screams.

Before she could react, Caro had pushed her aside, grabbed the shell and hurled it against the wall. It lay on the floor, cracked and splintered.

Stark hopelessness transmuted into fury and Madeleine screamed. She screamed into her daughter's face until her throat hurt. She didn't want to hold her, she didn't want to kiss her; she didn't want anything from her. She wanted to …

Caro was hunched against the wall with her hands over her ears. Madeleine glared at her and began to pick up the bits of shell. Inside the largest piece, something glinted.

The drawer was a mess of keys, screws and bits of metal. She scrunched up the Greenhaven letter in one hand as she felt around for a nail file. Ignoring the small figure against the wall, she prodded and coaxed until the object came away.

'Five for joy.' Caro had come to stand by her side.

The chased silver ring, beautiful in its simplicity, was slightly bent but still fitted her finger. Smoothing out the Greenhaven letter, Madeleine reached for the telephone.

# GREY SNAKES

It was starting again. She woke on a bed full of fur coats and lifted her head from the smell of must and perspiration. The familiar taste of rubber in her throat told her that she'd probably drunk too much and she prayed she had not been sick over the coats or in the open wardrobe to her left. She wiped away a smear of drool from her chin. Every muscle in her body cramped and released and the thing that was her head throbbed to the irregular beating of her heart.

Swallowing painfully, she passed one hand down her bodice and felt the grey snakes, writhing and encircling her waist. She blinked several times to clear her gaze. The room was large and airy. Strong disinfectant failed to mask the underlying smell of urine.

Her eyes swivelled to the cherubs, smirking and copulating, on the vaulted ceiling. One of them wore a stiff, white collar that dug into its fat neck. With two fingers it made the sign of the cross over her.

'This is my beloved daughter, in whom I am well pleased.'

'She's been out for too long this time.' A female cherub pursed rosy lips and frowned.

'Her mouth is foul with lies.'

'Further treatment could be dangerous.'

'You must save her immortal soul.'

Her eyes alighted on the barred window with heavy drapes. Whose party this time?

Sitting up, she wriggled her toes into soft, embroidered evening slippers. The heavy door handle yielded and she stepped out into the corridor. There was too-bright light and strange noises. The house, whoever's house it was, glittered with chandeliers and the laughter of a hundred people rose up from the floor below. At the top of the broad staircase was a liveried footman in a powdered wig. He held a tray of glasses.

He bowed low. 'Your medication, madam.'

Moving her tongue over the icy crispness of the champagne she smoothed her hair and, with a straight back, began to descend, slow by slow step. The hem of her dress glittered with tubular beads that brushed and tinkled against her ankles and as her fingers trailed down the banister, a hundred pairs of eyes swivelled to look. She recognized no one.

A cultured voice called: 'Andrea, my dear. Are you feeling better?'

'She's looking much better, Lady Dalton,' a man, dressed as a matador, whispered loudly behind his hand.

'I'm afraid I've been ill in your bedroom,' she said. 'Please forgive me.'

Lady Dalton, dressed as a nun, sipped a yellow cocktail covered in parasols. Her teeth were too large for her face and her bosoms strained against the black cloth.

'Please don't worry, Andrea. Take two of these pills and enjoy the party.'

'Thank you.' She moved away to talk to a small man slumped in a chair. He was wearing pyjamas and his face was half-covered with a parrot mask.

'I don't believe we've met,' she said, holding out her hand to be kissed. 'My name is Andrea.' That was right wasn't it? That's what Lady Dalton had called her?

'Piss off,' said the man and hid his face in a cushion.

A Strauss waltz began to play and a tall man wearing a monkey suit asked her to dance. His hair hung in greasy strands and his breath smelled of coffee. She moved awkwardly in his arms and he grimaced.

'They've been giving you too much, girl,' he said, peering into her eyes. 'Get the hell out of here.'

The music changed to a tango. A short man dressed as a priest came between them and took her in his arms.

'Are you ready to give yourself to God, my child?' His tongue flickered out like a lizard's.

She stared at his stiff collar and struggled as his podgy hands with their too-clean nails began to probe her buttocks. It was him!

Whirling around, she shook off his restraining arm and ran for the door. The guards had moved away for a moment and she was able to wrench it open and bolt out into the night. She raced across the courtyard and through deserted streets, slimy with rain.

'You shouldn't have told, Andrea.'

He was behind her and his voice sent shivers of disgust down her spine. As she ran, the grey snakes heaved their heavy coils and broke free of the embroidery on her dress. They dropped off one by one as she ducked into an alley and pressed herself against the wall. It was running with moisture and she could feel it seeping into her hair and into the back of her dress.

'Andreeea.' The voice was sly and wheedling and it was close.

She slid sideways along the wall, mashing the snakes into the cobbles. As her feet slid in the red mess, her slippers disintegrated and the rough stones at her back ripped away her brilliant gown. Barefoot and dressed only in a white shift, she saw an open window, high up in the wall to her right.

The nightmare always ended at this point. She closed her eyes, waiting to wake up.

'God wants you, Andrea.'

Stones dug into her naked back and her eyes snapped open.

He was almost upon her. His eyes were red pinpricks in the gloom. She launched herself forwards, bent her knees and flew upwards. With hands carved out of ice she scrabbled at the sill. His fingers caught at her heels. She kicked him in the face and squeezed her way through the narrow gap, slamming the window shut behind her.

Somehow, he floated in mid-air. Somehow, his face pressed against the glass. She could see blood pouring from his nose and staining the white collar. He was genuflecting and pretending to pray, but his voice was a venomous hiss.

'I warned you.'

Dropping down, she ran, her feet slapping the tiled floor. The corridor seemed to recede as she passed a door with a large, gold cross. Flames appeared and scorched words of Latin: *Ect su ite.* In this room they would force open her mouth. In this room, people screamed.

She was tiring. Aware of the fire building in her chest, she ran towards the bright light at the end of the corridor. In the shiny reflection of the metal door she could see him closing in on her.

'*Mea culpa. Mea maxima culpa.*' Through the words of contrition he was smiling. He reached inside his robes and held out an offering. The grey snake wriggled and stiffened. Its tongue shivered to a point. There was a bead of venom glistening at the tip.

She burst through the double doors and blinked in confusion.

Lady Dalton was walking towards her. She had changed her costume and was now wearing a blue dress and white cap.

'My dear! Father Michael has been praying on you.'

'Save me!'

'There now.' Lady Dalton took her arm in a grip of steel. The priest came up behind her and began choking her with his forearm. The grey snake forced its fangs deep into her thigh.

Everyone was laughing; the man in the monkey suit, the matador and the man with the parrot mask. 'It's for your own good,' they said, hiding their teeth behind their hands and ignoring her screams as she was dragged back down the corridor to the ECT suite.

'Vital signs?'
'She's gone.'
'There'll be an inquiry.'
'Call Father Michael.'
'Time of death 14.50.'

She woke on a bed of fur coats and looked at the barred window and the cherubs smirking on the vaulted ceiling. The one with a stiff, white collar held out its blood-soaked hands and the room reeked of the grave.

## *Grey Snakes*

She slipped her feet into embroidered evening slippers and rose wearily. Whose party this time?

# Rainbows of Maui

The wind coming in through the window riffled Lizzie's white cotton sunhat and she breathed in deeply, glad of the fresh air. There had been a very bad smell in the house. A maggot fell off her hat onto her skirt and she squished it absent-mindedly. The taxi driver glanced in the mirror, seeing a mousy little woman in drab middle-aged clothes. She had a sweet smile though.

'Nice day for it,' he said.

'It is, yes.'

The car moved smoothly into the flow of traffic heading for Heathrow and Lizzie reclined against the leather seat. It was indeed a very good day for it, long overdue but worth the wait.

'Terminal Three, love?'

'That's right.'

'Going somewhere nice?'

'Marbella.'

'Oh, you'll love it there. Me and the missus went two years ago. Cheap drinks, packed with Brits - we had a fantastic time.' He cut into the outside lane to the annoyance of several other drivers.

'Not going on your own are you?' he asked, ignoring the flashing headlights and tooting horns as he swerved back into the middle lane.

'Oh, no I'm going with a group. I'd never go on my own.'

'Very wise love, can't be too careful these days.'

They navigated the intricate roads around the airport and finally swept around in a circle, stopping with a flourish outside the doors of Terminal Three.

Lizzie took her case from the taxi driver. 'Thank you very much.'

'Will you be alright love?'

'Oh yes, thank you for your concern, but I can see some of my group inside.'

The taxi driver watched her for a moment, as she walked through the glass doors. Poor old thing - he hoped she had a good time in Spain, she looked as though she needed it.

As soon as she was inside the building, Lizzie straightened up and made purposefully for the nearest disabled toilet. A young man, leaning against one of the pillars, watched with narrowed eyes as the door closed behind her. He folded his arms and waited.

Laying her suitcase on the floor, she selected a few items and stood in front of the large mirror. She took off her cotton hat, revealing short golden-brown hair, which easily teased out into untidy, fashionable spikes. She scrutinised the cut and the colour with suspicious eyes and then relaxed.

The hair stylist at the top London salon had said it was the 'just got out of bed' look. It was worth every penny; she hadn't felt so young and confident in years. Edward would be horrified.

Smiling with satisfaction she started stripping off the floral dress and grey cardigan that Edward had chosen for her. He had chosen all her clothes and she had allowed it, pathetically grateful for the attention he gave her. Wanting to please him as she had always tried to please her father.

She stuffed the clothes into the bin and threw her sensible white cotton underwear on top. Reverently, she lifted up the scraps of oyster silk lingerie. They had also cost a fortune but, because they went on Edward's gold card, she had bought six sets. Her eyes widened as she did up the bra.

'Are those my breasts?'

She began to giggle as she pulled on a low cut, orange vest, purple silk trousers, loose jacket, and long floating scarf. Everything slithered over her skin and she shivered voluptuously. Slipping her feet into purple high-heeled sandals, she stood back to admire her reflection. She lightly applied make-up and sprayed herself with perfume. Heavy gold earrings and dark glasses completed the change.

She smiled at herself. 'Goodbye Lizzie - hello Nicole!'

She fastened the case with a decisive click.

Fifteen minutes later, she was sipping a glass of wine in the bar overlooking Arrivals. Her flight wasn't due for an hour and she had time to reflect on the past.

She had been working for a large firm of solicitors when she had met Edward, then a junior partner in the firm. She had been Nicole then, but Edward had preferred her second name.

'Elizabeth is an elegant name, so much more appropriate.'

Nicole gave in. But then everyone had started calling her Lizzie, and it stuck. She would have done anything to please Edward in those days.

As soon as they were married Edward had insisted that she give up work. So she became the dutiful wife and tried to make his overlarge, chilly house into a home for the family she longed for. After three miscarriages, Edward had told her to forget about 'this baby nonsense' and had bought her a Siamese kitten instead. Lizzie disliked cats. Steadily he moulded her into the wife that he wanted.

Nicole looked up as a young man walked over to the bar. Tall and handsome, with long dark hair, he gazed casually around until his eyes came to rest upon her. Then he smiled. She smiled back then looked away. She was old enough to be his mother - well maybe his older sister! Lizzie would have cringed but Nicole continued to smile as she sipped her wine.

Edward had taken her to various functions over the years, where all the other wives and girlfriends looked glamorous and confident while she felt uncomfortable in the shapeless dresses and flat sandals that he had chosen for her. He had kissed the top of her head and said, 'They look like tarts, Lizzie. You look elegant, classical - the perfect wife of a partner.' And she had smiled, glad of his approval.

It took her a while to realise that Edward was being unfaithful with one of those 'tarts'. Everybody else seemed to know and when she found out she was humiliated. He ended the affair and promised it would never happen again. It did though, again and again, and in the end she didn't really care.

She took an evening class in art at a local school and found that she was very good at it. When she transferred to a degree course at the London College of Art, she didn't tell Edward and he didn't notice.

'Off to your little class?' he would say.

It was while she was studying Textiles and Design that she had met Carl. A big, confident Australian, he made Lizzie nervous at first. Then they had to work together over an intricate garment, and they argued and laughed all week. They started to go out together on occasional evenings and quickly became known as 'the odd couple'. Carl became her best friend and was there when she was presented with her degree. She had been bereft when he'd gone abroad to start up a business.

Then, one day Edward came home and told her that he had found the love of his life, that he could not live without her and that he wanted a divorce.

'We're both adults, Lizzie,' he said, smoothing his beloved spoiled Siamese cat, draped smugly over his lap. 'Both mature people, so this can be done quickly and painlessly. I will settle a generous amount of money on you and you will be able to invest in a nice little flat for yourself. I, of course, will want the house as Sharon and I intend to start a family as soon as possible.'

He smiled as though expecting her to wish him congratulations.

'And of course,' he continued, 'Alfred likes this house, don't you boy?'

The cat yowled noisily, then spat at Lizzie.

She had met Sharon, who was half Edward's age, and seriously doubted that she would live up to his expectations of a wife.

'Of course,' she had murmured, turning away to hide her smile. 'I wish you every happiness, Edward.'

He had indeed been very generous but then, as she said to herself, she had earned it. She had banked the money and rented a flat. She told Edward that she needed a carpet, looking as pathetic as she could and he offered to pay for it if, in return she would look after Alfred and the house while he and Sharon went on honeymoon to Thailand.

He gave her his cash card and wagged his finger. 'I'm trusting you now, Lizzie.'

'Silly bugger!' She said out loud, laughing down her nose with derision.

'Pardon?' said the young man, in the act of sitting down. His voice had a foreign inflection.

She waved her hand airily and giggled. The man raised a speculative eyebrow and turned away.

She had shopped until she dropped and it had been an exhilarating experience. Floating silks, softest cashmere and slinky satins, all in vibrant, glowing colours - everything that poor Lizzie was not, and all paid for by an unsuspecting Edward.

Every day she withdrew large amounts of money until the account was drained. The money went into the expensive wallet, which went into the even more expensive bag along with her new passport under her new name, Nicole Overbury.

A large crowd milled out of Arrivals. Nicole leaned an elbow on the rail and scanned the faces with interest. After five minutes, she saw them. Edward, looking angry and impatient, was wheeling a baggage trolley, laden with suitcases. He stopped for a moment to mop his face with his handkerchief while his new wife, in high heels, tapped quickly ahead of him and was busy making eye contact with a young pilot.

Nicole grinned. 'Now I'm ready to congratulate you, Edward,' she said softly.

'That poor man.' Nicole jumped as her table companion spoke. 'He has had too much sun; his face is bright red. His woman, however, looks pleased with herself, that pilot has just slipped her his card.' He stood up and swept back his long dark hair with his fingers. 'Count Nicholas Grazinski, how do you do?' He bowed slightly and held out his hand and Nicole found herself laughing and putting her hand in his.

'Nicole Overbury, I'm pleased to meet you Count Grazinski.' His lips felt warm against her hand.

'You will permit me to buy you a drink?' The lines at the side of his mouth deepened into a smile. He really was very attractive, she thought and slid her dark glasses down to look at him.

'Your eyes ... ' she said.

'Yes?'

'They're most unusual.'

'A family trait; all Grazinski males have one blue, one green eye. This disturbs you?'

'Not at all, they're quite ... beautiful.' She removed her glasses and held his gaze.

He hesitated, then turned and almost tripped as he made his way to the bar. Nicole stretched and purred with pleasure; she was enjoying herself and it was about time.

He came back with the drinks and Nicole gave him a brilliant smile.

'The carpet looked fantastic!' she said.

He frowned. 'This is a code, no?'

She laughed as she sipped her drink and gazed at the throng below.

'Would passengers waiting to board flight 373 to Hawaii please make their way to gate seventeen.'

Her companion got to his feet, blew her a kiss with his fingers and was gone.

Nicole reached for her bag and scrabbled around in disbelief - it had gone!

She panicked and began to tremble. Lizzie was starting to return. Nicole stood up and squared her shoulders. No way was she going back to being that frightened little mouse!

She walked purposefully down the stairs, looking all around and then she saw him. She strode towards gate seventeen, pushed her way through the queue and tapped him on the shoulder.

'Count Grazinski? I believe you have something of mine?'

He handed her the clutch bag without a word and she hit him

over the head with it before being swept up into his arms and whirled around in a bear hug. The other passengers looked on in amazement.

'Just making sure you weren't going to change your mind, babe.'

The Australian drawl was sweet to her ears.

'Carl, you idiot! You frightened the life out of me!'

'Got to keep you on your toes girl, you've become rusty!' He draped an arm around her shoulder as they moved forward. 'Remember those nights when we used to go out and pretend we were different people?'

Nicole laughed. 'I remember the night you asked me to come as Madonna.'

'Yeah - and you came dressed as the Virgin Mary! Not quite what I had in mind. You look fabulous by the way, one of your designs?'

She nodded and put her arm around his waist.

'You didn't have to come and get me,' she said later as they walked onto the plane. 'I'd have managed.'

'I know you would, but I had business to see to in London and I've found the most amazing fabrics, just wait till you see them, you'll drool!'

Nicole sat down by the window. 'Business still taking off then?'

'And how! Fantasy wear, fancy dress - they can't get enough of it! I'm having to beat them off with a stick. And now that you're on board, it'll be better than ever.' He clicked his seat belt shut and reached over to squeeze her hand. 'I've really missed you, babe.'

Nicole turned her head and smiled into his strange eyes. 'Is Maui as beautiful as you described in your letters?'

He became serious. 'Much more beautiful. There's a lagoon that I'm going to take you to. It has a waterfall and you can swim underneath and if you blow through the water, you can make little rainbows. It's paradise, Nicole.'

As the plane began its ascent, she looked down at the houses below and a small smile played around her mouth.

'Don't you wish now that you'd taken revenge on Edward?' Carl looked at her curiously.

'I'm not like that.' Nicole said primly. But Lizzie was, and inside she was grinning from ear to ear!

Edward and his bride would be arriving home just about now. He would be turning the key in the lock and he might even, if he had the strength, make the grand gesture and carry his bride over the threshold into the house that had been Lizzie's home for twenty years. She did so hope that they would like the changes she had made.

Alfred had gone first. She had put an ad in the paper: 'Free to good home: pedigree, sealpoint Siamese', and he was snapped up in the first two days by a fierce-looking woman who lived fifty miles away.

Lizzie bought fresh pork, chicken giblets and fish and inserted them into every crack and crevice that she could find; down the backs of the leather sofa and chairs, in small slits in the bridal bed, in the hollow curtain rails and down the backs of all the kitchen cupboards. She switched the central heating full on, then went out and sat in the sunny garden with all the windows and doors open and smiled as she watched the flies pour in. She left the bathroom alone except for the new toothbrushes. She carefully took them out of their packaging and methodically and earnestly cleaned under the rim of the lavatory and all around the cat litter tray with them before replacing them in their packets.

The Aubisson though, gave her the greatest pleasure. It was Edward's pride and joy and had cost a small fortune. She had seen him on numerous occasions, stooping to pick a minute piece of fluff from the thick pile of the gold and turquoise carpet. Lizzie had bought several packets of Rocket cress seeds and had sown them all over the carpet to the raucous strains of 'Bat out of Hell'. Every day, she had watered them and in three days had been rewarded with a living floor of inch high moss.

Good luck with your new wife Edward, she thought serenely, because you'll never hear from Lizzie again. She gave a great sigh and held her friend's hand for luck as the plane banked, climbed and flew them away to paradise.

## Sailing By

On a dark night, high above a small seaside town, a storm gathered and broke; while on the coastal path, oblivious to the torrential rain, two lovers argued. The boy reached for the girl's hand only to have it snatched away. A sudden flash of lightning illuminated her swollen belly as she stamped her foot and turned to run away. The boy caught her as she fell.

The iron fish gaped at me as I grasped the head and brought it down with a crack against the door. At that same moment, thunder echoed overhead and my hair lifted with static as I held on to the door knocker. I stared at my hand - white, and running with rainwater. It was the hand of a stranger.

With a suddenness that made me jump, the heavy door was flung open. A plump woman stood illuminated in the hallway, light glinting on her glasses and making a halo of her white hair.

'I'm Mrs. Evans,' she said, pushing her glasses to the top of her head and reaching for my hand. 'I've been expecting you. Oh, will you look at all that weather! Come in, come in love, you're soaked.'

She pulled me inside and closed the door. 'Come far have you?' Without waiting for a reply, she drew me down the passage and into the kitchen.

'There now, sit down here by the fire and have a warm. Kettle's on.'

I sat down in the worn leather chair and stared at the water pooling around my bare feet, while Mrs. Evans bustled about, clattering cups and humming under her breath.

I looked around me and saw whitewashed walls with framed

photographs massed around, a flagstone floor with colourful rag rugs and two old easy chairs either side of the glowing fire. A large, scrubbed table stood in the centre of the room together with a mismatched assortment of wooden chairs. Against the far wall stood a gleaming Welsh dresser, sagging with china, baby photographs and small brass ornaments.

How did I get here? Why did I need to get here? My heart began to pound as I remembered the feeling of urgency but not the purpose. I put a hand to my aching forehead.

'Here we go.' She was by my side, holding out a faded blue towel.

I rubbed my hair with shaking fingers and pressed my face into the fragrance of sun and sea air. I must be ill, that was it. If I could just stay here for a little while, I felt sure I would remember everything. The clock ticked steadily as I forced myself to relax.

'Don't you worry now,' she said as if reading my mind. 'You can stay here for as long as you want.' She placed a flower-sprigged cup and saucer on the black leaded grate at my side. 'We'll have some bread and cheese in a bit - my own bread that's just come out of the oven - lovely and crusty it is, though I say so myself. Now, I've put a couple of hot water bottles in your bed so it's all ready for you, whenever you want to go up.' She patted my shoulder. 'Poor little mite, you're exhausted.'

I sipped my tea and watched her plump figure bustling about the kitchen. Warmth began to course through my body as I lay back in my chair. I must have slept for a while and I stretched luxuriously when Mrs. Evans called over.

'Come and try some of this, it'll buck you up no end.'

I sat down at the table as she started to cut generous slices of crusty bread, spreading them liberally with butter and slices of golden cheese.

'Alright?'

I nodded blissfully, my mouth full.

'More cheese?'

'Mmm!'

She smiled, pleased. 'That's what I like - a good appetite.' She helped herself to another slice. 'I don't like to see these poor young things with arms like sticks. Not like me. Mr. Evans used to say that he sometimes thought I liked my food better than him and most of the time he was right!' She laughed, patting her stomach.

As she began to collect the dishes she saw me looking at the photographs on the wall.

'That's my family.'

Family? The room rocked as my anxiety returned.

'My Grandfather Thomas,' she said, indicating a large sepia photograph of a man in a dark naval uniform. 'Sea captain he was, one of the first Cape Horners, lost three fingers on his left hand. That's my Granny May.' A prim version of Mrs. Evans stared out, a cameo at her starched collar, her hand resting lightly on her husband's shoulder. 'Lovely she was, brought me up.'

'Who's this?' I managed to point to a smiling young woman in an elegant dress.

Mrs. Evans sighed. 'My mother. Died when I was a baby.'

I scraped back my chair. 'I feel sick!'

'Alright, take your time now.' She led me by the hand to the easy chair and the fire burst into life as she stabbed and lifted the coals in the grate. 'Had a time of it you have, and there's me going on and on.'

She began to sweep the scattered breadcrumbs from the cloth and looked at me. 'It will be alright, you know, whatever you decide to do.'

I leaned my head back against the soft cushions and closed my eyes. I could hear her moving about, could hear the soft chink of china; then light began to move and pulse against my eyelids. A shaft of light swept past the window. I blinked. Another shaft, followed by another. The room lurched. Sounds that burbled like voices underwater suddenly became clear.

'*We had a row ... Distress ... Foetal heartbeat ... Do something! ... Calm down sir, we're going as fast as ...*'

I jumped as the door opened. Mrs. Evans came back in through a small outer door, her hair blown about her head.

'Wind's getting up something dreadful. I've checked the light - we don't want a nasty accident, and I've seen some I can tell you, living here all these years.'

For the first time I realized that the room was entirely round as the light swept past the window again.

She squashed the kettle down onto the fire with firm circular movements. 'Well I think you've got a bit more colour in your cheeks now. What do you say, Tibs?' She spoke to a large, striped tabby cat that had appeared by the side of my chair. He meowed and leapt lightly onto my lap.

I smiled at Mrs. Evans, who had sat down in the opposite chair with a contented sigh and had started knitting something small and pink. Tibs purred, the clock ticked and my eyelids drooped.

'Time to go?'

I started. 'What do you mean?' Anxiety pounded in my throat.

'I said, do you want to go up to bed, dear? It'll be lovely and warm by now.'

I longed for sleep, but it was comforting to be by the fire, watching Mrs. Evans counting her stitches.

She peered at me over her glasses. 'There now, no rush. You stay by there for a bit and keep me company.'

Her needles clicked and the little garment grew at an amazing rate as my eyes closed. I heard the coals settle on the fire and, through my eyelids, swooping shafts of light hypnotised me.

*'Blood pressure two hundred over one-ten ... Do something! ... She's fitting! ... Oh, please God, no! ... Prep for theatre ... Crash!'*

I jumped, and the cat leapt off my lap, spitting.

'Oh, sorry love, but I need to hear the shipping forecast.'

I could hear the crackle of a radio as Mrs. Evans deftly cast off and reached for a notebook and pencil.

'End of the news, thank goodness,' she said, opening the notebook. 'Nothing but doom and gloom these days.'

'I hate anger,' I said. 'I cannot bear it.'

Mrs. Evans rifled through the pages of her book until she found the right page. 'Oh, I don't know. Mr. Evans and I used to argue all the time,' she said.

I stared at her, horrified.

She flapped the book at me and laughed. 'He used to say if we didn't have a good row, the day was spoiled.' She twinkled at me over her glasses. 'Mind you, the making up was always sweet.'

As I digested this, a signature tune started on the radio.

'"Sailing By" - my favourite bit of music.' Mrs. Evans licked the tip of her pencil as a man started speaking.

*'Here is the shipping forecast ... Stand clear! ... Warning of gales in all areas ... And again, clear please! ... expected in Scotland 0700 hours tomorrow ... Oh, dear God, please!'*

I sat up straight in my chair. 'I think I'm ready now, Mrs. Evans.'

She looked up. 'Alright, dear. In your own time.'

*'Dogger, becoming cyclonic, backing East.'*

Mrs. Evans tutted.

*'South, South West, White, Portland ... Infant flat!'*

Mrs. Evans' pencil flew across the page.

*'No breaths! ... Lundy, Fastnet, severe force nine.'*

'I will go now, Mrs. Evans.' My voice was stronger as I stood up.

'Alright then, cariad,' she said. 'You know the way.'

In the recovery room, the young man watched his wife being wheeled through the double doors. His face was the colour of her sheet as he wrapped thin arms about himself and shivered. A nurse in the dark blue uniform of a sister watched him from the doorway. She went over and he jumped as she touched his arm.

'Your wife will be fine now,' she said. 'Let them give her a wash and put her into a clean nightdress, then you can go in to see her.'

He nodded, unable to speak.

Her voice became brisk. 'You haven't held baby yet, have you? Sit down and I'll bring her to you.'

He stepped back. 'No! I mean she's so small. I don't think I should, not yet.'

The nurse settled him firmly in a chair. 'I think you could both do with a cuddle, don't you?'

He pushed nervous fingers through his hair and wiped his hands on his jeans as she came back.

'Here we are.'

His face was rigid as she placed the bundle in his arms. He held the baby awkwardly and gazed into eyes that were the colour of the ocean. Suddenly, a tiny starfish hand snared his little finger.

'My daughter,' he whispered, looking up into the kindly face of the nurse. Holding the baby close, he kissed her and fell in love for only the second time in his young life.

And I, safe in the arms of my father, closed my eyes and slept.

## Once Bitten

I woke up scratching furiously. I must have been bitten during the night. A group of noisy revellers went past in the street below as I closed the window and stumbled to the bathroom. High up on my inner thigh the skin was red where I had been digging at it with my nails. The lump was small, no larger than a seed but it itched abominably. I blinked hard to clear my vision. Was it ... ? Oh God, the thing was moving.

I found a razor blade and sliced my skin. It stung and blood welled up but the itching maddened me, so I dug the blade in deeper. There was a sudden, strong smell of aniseed and to my horror two black feelers appeared, followed by a raisin-like body. I cried out in revulsion as a spider burst free and sprang to the floor. Retching, I felt a second break through, then a third. Outside, another group of laughing people went past. They didn't hear my screams.

Convinced I would die unless I got them all out, I worked my finger into the wound until it was gaping open. Dozens of spiders, slick with blood, dropped to the floor where they formed a rustling circle around my feet. They began to bite. Gagging and sobbing I stamped them into a vortex of stinking, red-brown mush.

Fingers snapped at my ear. I woke to the sound of laughter and saw nightmarish faces, red with excitement.

'How are you feeling?' A man with a bad hairpiece and breath that stank of aniseed gleamed at me. 'You can go back to your seat, dear ... for now.' He winked at the audience. 'Give the lady a big hand, folks.'

I stared around at the packed theatre and flinched at the gaping mouths and pointing fingers. There were several people slumped in chairs behind me.  They appeared to be sleeping.  The laughter increased as I brought my gaze back to the man and struggled to focus.  There was something ...

He took my elbow to guide me off the stage but I hung back, staring at a small lump in the inner corner of his left eye.  It was starting to move.  My fingers closed around the nail file in the pocket of my dress.